CLIMAX

Love in London, Book 3

LAUREN SMITH

Copyright © 2016 by Lauren Smith

This book was Previously Published in 2016 by Hachette Book Group USA and is now republished by Lauren Smith Books in 2018

Cover design by Cover Couture

Stock Photography: Shutterstock/Botond Horvath & Depositphotos/Yurkaimmortal

ISBN: 978-1-947206-66-3 (ebook)

ISBN: 978-1-947206-47-2 (Trade paperback)

❀ Created with Vellum

A Gentleman Never Surrenders
A Scottish Lord for Christmas

Contemporary
The Surrender Series
The Gilded Cuff
The Gilded Cage
The Gilded Chain
The Darkest Hour
Love In London
Forbidden
Seduction
Climax
Forever Be Mine

Paranormal
Dark Seductions Series
The Shadows of Stormclyffe Hall
The Love Bites Series
The Bite of Winter
Brothers of Ash and Fire
Grigori
Mikhail
Rurik

Sci-Fi Romance
Cyborg Genesis Series
Across the Stars

1

"They're not going to find out about us." A deep masculine voice cut through Kat Roberts's muddled thoughts.

She jerked her gaze away from the street view through the town house's kitchen window. It didn't feel like home, but it was her father's fiancée's house, and she would be coming here for future holidays while studying at Cambridge. She would have to get used to it, even the servants appearing around the corner unexpectedly. Maybe after a while it would feel like home if she spent enough time here.

"Kat." That voice, with its sexy British accent, was the reason she'd gotten into this mess. That voice and its owner were completely irresistible, impossibly seductive.

A tall, dark, and sexy dream. No woman could resist that. She hadn't been able to. Since their kiss in the middle of a pub one snowy night, she'd been falling hopelessly in love with him more and more each passing day. With a man she couldn't have.

Tristan Kingsley. He was a twenty-five-year-old bad boy, a business student at Cambridge, and the future Earl of

Pembroke. He was a heartbreaker, and she couldn't stay out of his bed. But most importantly, he was her future step-brother. Her father had just gotten engaged to his mother, and they were planning their wedding, much to Kat's and Tristan's dismay.

If Dad finds out I've been sleeping with my future stepbrother...

Tristan cleared his throat. "Don't worry. I promise no one will know."

When she looked his way, her mouth went dry and her tongue stuck to the roof of her mouth, making it hard to form words. He always had that effect on her, and she finally understood that expression about a man being a tall drink of water. He made her thirsty just looking at him.

He was leaning one hip against the kitchen counter, arms crossed over his chest. The black trousers showed off his long, muscled legs, and the white dress shirt he wore was unrestrained by a tie, the open collar revealing his throat. She loved to grip that collar when she dragged his head down for a kiss. She glimpsed the sensitive patch of skin she'd spent last night kissing because it made his hips jerk when he was inside her. But her feelings for him were so much more than just physical.

There was something about him, the way he stood at ease, yet every part of his body was hard as steel, like he carried the burden of the responsibility for others on his shoulders. Tristan tried to hide that part of himself when he was with her, but she sensed it was never far from the surface. His sculpted features were undeniable in their beauty and brought to life by his intense, often quiet study of the world around him. He had an air that said he was a cut above others, but what she'd thought was arrogance was actually confidence. She loved that he wasn't afraid to be himself in a world that put too much pressure on a person being someone they weren't. His strength gave her strength, too, which was something she desperately needed after yesterday.

When they'd gone to Harrods to buy a Christmas tree for his mother's town house, paparazzi had tracked Tristan down inside the store. Kat had been overwhelmed by the flashing cameras and questions shouted, but Tristan had kept his calm, and they'd hidden in a broom closet until the reporters lost them.

She'd tasted the pressures of Tristan's position and the nonstop involvement of the news in his personal life. It was apparent that she didn't fit into his glittering world of titled men and women with grand estates, lofty expectations, and an existence that was open to public scrutiny.

Yet when they kissed...well, it was a case of a match meeting a keg of gunpowder, and all the fears and worries of not belonging with him faded away. She just went up in flames whenever he touched her. No man had ever made her feel so wild...so alive. She couldn't walk away from him, even knowing how risky their situation was. She and Tristan weren't blood related, but her dad would freak out if he found his nineteen-year-old daughter sleeping with a man like Tristan. He was a notorious playboy who'd broken hearts and spent nights in the beds of some of London's most famous bachelorettes.

He was her sex god. The man who made every hot, wild fantasy come true. And she was not supposed to be with him.

It was a nightmare.

"What are we going to do?" Kat slumped into a chair at the kitchen table. The house was quiet this early in the morning, except for the occasional creaks and groans of the wood settling.

"We'll explain the photos, but we'll keep the truth about us buried." Tristan pushed away from the counter and took the chair beside her. It seemed so easy for him to talk about hiding their relationship. She knew he didn't take this as seriously as she did. She was falling in love with him, but he wasn't in love with her. This was more of a game for him, a sexy game of hide-and-seek. But the stakes were too high now. Their dirty little secret had just gone public because of the photos.

The photos.

If only there hadn't been evidence, they might've kept their relationship secret a little while longer. A photographer named Jillian had talked them into portraying Snow White and Prince Charming in a fairy-tale-themed charity photo competition at Harrods department store. The set had been lifelike, a glass coffin shimmering with frost and snow. She'd rested her head on a white satin pillow and lay waiting for Tristan to kiss her awake. As magical as that experience had been for her, the fallout had been worse than she could have imagined.

The photographer had led them to believe the winning photo would not be made public and that the stills would be seen only in her portfolio. Early this morning, the winner had been announced on TV. Their photo in a snowy glen, their mouths a hairsbreadth apart from a kiss, their eyes locked in desire and longing, with SOME LOVES LAST FOREVER beneath them, was going to be plastered on every flat surface in London from bus stops to billboards.

How would she explain this to her dad? The last thing Kat wanted to do was create a problem between her father and Tristan's mom.

"Did you call Jillian?" she asked Tristan.

"I did call her. She said it would blow over soon. She didn't think they'd do a news feature about it." Tristan scrubbed a hand though his dark hair and sighed. "Maybe we'll get lucky and Prince Harry will visit Las Vegas again and the press will chase him for a bit and lose interest in us." Tristan's laugh was hollow.

Her heart gave a little tug inside her chest. He looked defeated and anxious. From the moment she'd met him, he'd been cool and seductive and playful. A force of nature in some ways. Nothing had cut through that hardened bad-boy exterior.

Until me. She'd pushed him away twice, trying to deny the intense attraction between them, but she'd only made them both miserable. She'd decided that being with Tristan was worth all the consequences, so she'd asked him to come home from his father's estate. They'd spent all night in bed. It was the kind of lovemaking that changed a person's life forever.

Then they'd woken up to this nightmare. Jillian's photo was everywhere, and the story was out. Their parents would connect the dots.

"We'll tell them a half-truth." Tristan reached under the table and placed a reassuring hand on her thigh. It was a sensual touch, but she could see in his eyes he wasn't thinking about sex.

The wildfire that burned between them was unstoppable, and the intensity had deepened in a way she'd never imagined. The attraction that had drawn her to him like a moth to a flame was growing. Her beautiful, brooding Tristan, with his guarded heart, was trying to comfort her. It wasn't just about sex anymore. Even if he didn't love her, he cared for her, and that was enough for now. And that was why she adored him, because even though the lust burning between them was unrelenting, he also cared about her, proving that he wasn't just thinking about sex, not when she was worried about other things.

How do we get out of this mess?

"What will we tell them?"

"We couldn't say no to a charity event. We just did what

the photographer told us to." He leaned over and pressed his lips against her neck. Tiny waves of comfort from that slow, tender brush of his mouth overrode her panic, if only for a moment. Tristan's kisses made her fall through time and space until she lost herself in his private universe.

"I'll tell them first thing. If we're open about it, they won't think we're hiding anything. Trust me, Kat." He cupped her face, and just like that, she was trapped in his blue-green gaze.

"I trust you." And she did.

"Good." He pressed a featherlight kiss to her lips, then jerked away as the kitchen door opened.

Tristan's mother, Lizzy, stood there, eyes darting between the two of them. Her long blond hair was pulled back in a fashionable chignon and she was dressed for the cold weather, her gloves damp with snow and her boots shiny with water.

"Tristan! When did you get back? I thought you were going to stay with Edward for the remainder of the holidays."

"Well, I was half-tempted to tell Father to stuff it, but then I decided I didn't care to speak to him about it all and just came back here without telling him. I'd much rather be with you for Christmas."

Lizzy's shoulders dropped in relief. "I hope your father doesn't get too angry."

They all hoped that. Tristan's coldhearted father was continually dragging Tristan home to the Pembroke estate whenever it suited him, regardless of Tristan's plans. He'd risked his father's fury coming home earlier than he promised, and Kat still feared that Tristan would suffer for it.

"I saw the most unusual...photograph this morning." Lizzy's face turned red as her gaze darted to Kat and then back to her son, betraying the nature of her thoughts. She fidgeted slightly, her lips parting as she licked them nervously.

Kat blinked, then swallowed hard as she took in Lizzy's

attire and realized Lizzy must've already gone out, which meant she had seen...

Tristan stood, smoothed his sweater, and offered his mother a smile. "You saw the charity photograph, didn't you? You see, it's quite the story. Kat and I were Christmas tree shopping, and a photographer begged us to be models for the shoot. We felt obligated to aid her, for charity, of course. Isn't that right, Kat?" His tone implied she ought to join in their little game of secrets.

Secrets. She hated them, but she wanted Tristan, at any cost.

Kat got to her feet, keeping a safe distance from Tristan, even though she wanted to reach for his hand.

"Yes. Jillian was very sweet. We couldn't turn her down, even when she told us we'd have to reenact Snow White. We're happy she won the contest. There were two other photographers involved in the fairy-tale photo shoots." She did her best not to sound too falsely excited.

"Oh?" Lizzy's voicing of that one syllable seemed to be a challenge—not a threatening one, but a worried one.

"Yes, the whole situation was far too awkward, but we endured it for the sake of charity, didn't we, Kat?" Tristan walked over to the fridge as he spoke and retrieved a pitcher of orange juice, calmly pouring himself a glass.

Lying seemed so easy for him, but it wasn't for her. Her palms got sweaty and she licked her lips every time Lizzy looked at her.

"Well, it was certainly nice of you to help with something that goes toward a good cause." Lizzy continued to stare at Kat, her brow furrowed, apparently deep in thought, but she was stopped from saying anything further when Kat's father strolled into the kitchen.

He was smiling and humming.

"Only one day until Christmas," he announced, and

leaned over to press a kiss to Lizzy's cheek before he hugged Kat. "Morning, sweetheart." Then he nodded at Tristan. "Tristan, back from your father's for Christmas?"

"Yes. I got in late last night and didn't want to wake anyone." Tristan inclined his head; then his gaze darted to Kat.

"Everyone have their shopping done?" Clayton asked.

Lizzy cleared her throat. "Actually, I need to grab a few things. Kat, would you like to join me?"

"Mum, I could take you—" Tristan took a small step toward his mother, as though to protect Kat from her.

"I'd love to go," Kat said. With a hand on Tristan's hip, she nudged him aside. He moved reluctantly. If she had to pick a parent to be around for the next few hours, Lizzy was a lot less scary than her dad when it came to keeping her secrets.

"Kat, how much time do you need to get ready? I'm able to leave as soon as you are." Lizzy already held a casual black clutch purse in one hand.

"A few minutes. I just need to grab my shopping list." She glanced at her father and then Tristan before bolting for the door.

Heart racing, she ran up the stairs and slid to a halt just inside the room. Blood pounded in her head, drumming against her temples. Keeping secrets had never been a talent of hers. She'd never had actual secrets to safeguard before, and now she had the mother of all secrets building into a violent storm inside her.

The question was, who would survive the fallout?

She'd taken two steps farther into her room, when a hand settled on her waist from behind and she sucked in a little shriek. Another hand clamped around her mouth, cutting off the sound. A tall, lean, muscled body pressed against her back.

"Shh...You have to calm down, Kat." Tristan's too-sexy

accented voice rumbled against her right ear, his breath tickling the fine hairs on her skin. He was so warm...and hard behind her. The pounding of his heart tapped against her back between the thin layer of their clothes, and she felt that inexorable pull toward him.

Like gravity. God, the man was the personification of sinful temptation. She never stood a chance.

He dropped his hand from her mouth. He dominated her whenever he touched her, and she craved that more than anything. She leaned back against him, absorbing his heat and strength. Being with him, even secretly, made her feel so alive, so feminine and sexy, but it wasn't just about the sex.

From the start she and Tristan had been connected on a level she'd never thought possible. It hadn't been love at first sight—she didn't believe in that—but it had been obsession at first sight. Something about him pulled her in, like a whirlpool in the Amazon River, drawing her deeper and deeper into him. Now she was unable and unwilling to escape. He'd let her have a glimpse into his soul, and she'd fallen hard and fast. It was a dangerous thing to be in love with Tristan Kingsley.

He shut her bedroom door and flicked the lock before leaning back against the closed door. When he crooked one finger in silent invitation, she closed the small distance between them. Tristan's arms wound around her waist as he tugged her tight to his body and dipped his head.

The slight pause before he kissed her was sensual torture. She wanted his mouth on hers, and he loved to tease her, make her wait even a second more than she wanted to. When his gaze traveled from her eyes down to her lips, she rocked up on her tiptoes, kissing him first like she had the night in the pub when they'd met.

Kat drank in the taste of him as their lips met. Electricity pulsed beneath her skin, humming softly with every feathery caress of his mouth on hers. She couldn't help but think of that line from *Romeo and Juliet* "Thus with a kiss I die..." How true it felt. This kiss stopped her heart for a second too long, and she spiraled into a world of need and hunger that knew no limits. There was no life outside his kiss.

A shiver of longing rippled through her. She needed more...and she needed fewer clothes.

Tugging at his pants, she tried to undo the button on his fly while still kissing him. His hands slid from her waist to her ass, gripping it hard. Spikes of sharp arousal tore through her, and her clit throbbed in little pulses of desire.

"You don't have to go with my mum." He flicked his tongue into her ear and she shivered. "You could stay right here..." Tristan let his words hang in the air with sensual promise as he rocked his hips, pressing against her hands, which were trying to open his pants. There were a hundred things he could do to convince her to stay right where she was, but his words reminded her that Lizzy was downstairs waiting for her. The thought brought her out of the sensual haze she'd been in, and she pulled away from him. Catching her breath, she shook her head, feeling foolish that he always derailed her when she was trying to be on her best behavior.

"As tempted as I am, I should go. I haven't bought your present yet and Christmas is tomorrow."

Tristan chuckled and rubbed a palm on her stomach. "The only present I want is you unwrapped beneath me in my bed." He kissed her cheek and held on to her for a long moment.

Kat clung to him. "I'd like that a lot, but I do *need* to shop. Spending time with your mom might be a good thing for both of us."

He pulled back so he could stare down at her. "We haven't talked much about our parents' upcoming marriage." He tipped her chin up with one elegant finger, and Kat bit her lip before replying. It stunned her that he had the power to turn a moment focused on sex to something packed with emotion. From the second he'd walked into the pub a few weeks ago, she felt as if she was riding on an emotional roller coaster.

"I'm coping, barely." Her mother had cut and run on her and her dad so long ago that she didn't know how to have a bigger family. "What about you?" she asked. Tristan had always been cool, calm, and collected, almost satirical in his approach to their parents, but he had to be hurting like she was.

For a brief instant, that wall of imperial control descended on his face, but then he softened. "Mum and I...aren't used to sharing each other. I've been the man of the house for a long time, and it's been disconcerting to relinquish most of that control to your father."

"It's definitely not easy to share a parent when you haven't had to before." She snuggled close again. "At least we have each other." The words slipped out before she could stop them.

Tristan made a soft dark noise and leaned down to kiss her hard, in an almost punishing manner before he spoke. "We *do* have each other, and you can't ever leave me again. Do you understand?"

She took in his face, the panic in his eyes and the tension bracketing his mouth. He'd been wounded when she'd called off their relationship. It seemed ironic that she'd gone into this thinking she'd be the one to get hurt, but instead she was the one causing him pain.

"I understand. I'm sorry, Tristan." The words caught in her throat and choked her.

He brushed at her cheeks, and she blushed when his fingertips came away wet with tears. Tristan made a teasing *tsk* noise before pressing another fervent kiss to her lips.

"So you and Mum will go shopping. What am I supposed to do while you're gone?"

She rolled one shoulder in a small shrug. "Bond with my dad?"

His rich laugh warmed her. "Not bloody likely, darling." He was still shaking his head with apparent amusement. "I'll plan something so you and I might have time alone later. How does that sound?"

Pretending to think about it for a minute, she finally nodded and then flashed him a grin. "Sounds nice."

"Excellent." He stole one more quick kiss before he slipped out of her bedroom.

That was the most important thing. Not getting caught together by their parents. Stepsiblings shouldn't be seen making out, and they definitely should not be having hot sex with each other...and she and Tristan had done both.

Dad would kill us if he found out...

2

A few minutes after Tristan left her room, Kat did the same. She could hear Tristan's voice echo up from the stairs. It sounded like he was talking to her father. She heard the word *Super Bowl* and rolled her eyes.

Her father was a football junkie. No one would know it to look at him; he was a polished, well-dressed investment banker, but when it came to football, he was one step away from painting his face and waving a giant foam finger.

Lizzy met her at the bottom of the stairs, smiling warmly. "The boys are occupied with sports, so we can make our escape."

"I'm ready to take on the last-minute Christmas shopping," she said, grinning as she followed Lizzy out the door.

Tristan's mother smiled back. "Me too. Let's hope the crowds aren't too terrible."

A black Porsche SUV was parked outside, and a driver in a black uniform opened the door as they walked down the slick sidewalk. They climbed into the car and buckled up.

"Where to, Ms. Harlow?" the driver asked as he started the car.

"Paul, take us to Harrods. We're on the hunt for an Aspinal of London briefcase."

The driver glanced at them through the rearview mirror. He was a ruddy-cheeked man who smiled at her. "Of course, my lady."

Lizzy settled her purse on her lap and glanced in Kat's direction as she tugged her black leather gloves off and slipped them into her purse.

For several long minutes neither of them spoke, but Kat couldn't stand the silence. "So, Lizzy..." She cleared her throat. "You need to do some last-minute shopping, too?"

Lizzy smiled. "Yes. I was hoping you might weigh in on a briefcase for your father. I noticed his is a little worse for wear. I was thinking of getting him a new one." She waited for Kat to respond, but the Porsche came to a halt in front of Harrods.

"Oh my..." Lizzy put one hand to her breast as she peered out the window at something.

"What?" Kat leaned toward her, able to see the bottom half of...She sucked in a breath.

The picture of her as Snow White and Tristan as Prince Charming covered an entire side of the department store. A picture that still caused heat to rush to her face and made her light-headed all at once, because it was obvious to anyone looking at that picture that she was in love with Tristan Kingsley. Kat hoped he felt the same about her, that he *loved* her.

"Paul, we'll call when we're ready to be picked up." Lizzy's voice was strangely quiet.

"Very good, my lady," Paul replied before he climbed out and opened their door.

Kat reached the sidewalk and tilted her head back to get a better glimpse of the huge ad.

"Well, that's quite a picture." Lizzy tugged her coat up

around her neck. "I imagine it was an interesting experience to shoot."

She nodded. "We were ambushed by the photographer and she talked us into posing for charity. So we did." Was it pathetic to admit, even to herself, how much she loved looking at the photo? *How did I fall in love with him so fast?* She'd always lived her life cautiously and kept most people at a distance.

Because Tristan wouldn't let me keep my distance. He opened me up and he opened himself up, and now look at us.

"What's the matter, Kat?" Lizzy touched her shoulder, and she came back to herself.

"Sorry. I'm just thinking, I need to get you and Tristan both presents. I hadn't planned for this." Damn, that hadn't come out right. "What I mean was, I didn't know about you until after I'd bought my presents a month ago." She hoped Lizzy understood what she was trying to say.

"It's fine, Kat. None of us planned this. I need to get you a gift as well." Lizzy smiled and squeezed Kat's shoulder. "If you see anything you like, just give me a wink and a nudge."

It was *impossible* to dislike Lizzy. Even though she was still struggling to accept the whole marriage thing, Kat couldn't deny how much she liked the woman her father had chosen.

"Same here—for you, I mean," she added, feeling a little shy but strangely excited. It had been so long since she'd been around a mother. Lizzy wasn't *her* mother, but shopping, just the two of them for a family Christmas, might actually be fun.

"Let's get inside. I'm thinking we should look for brief-cases first."

They entered the department store, pushing through the almost frantic crush of holiday shoppers to get to the escalators that would take them to their desired floors. Over the next hour she and Lizzy shopped, not just for the men but for each other and for themselves. They tried on fancy dresses and scarves, even *oohed* and *ahhed* over designer purses, things Kat never thought she'd do, much less enjoy doing. Yet Lizzy had coaxed her into dressing rooms and insisted she try on a dozen things just because she could.

It was *fun*.

Kat bought a blue linen photo album for their wedding photos and any others Lizzy might like to keep. She'd caught Lizzy admiring the album earlier and had a feeling it would be perfect.

Laden with purchases, they met Paul at the car and he dutifully relieved them of their bags and packages, stowing them methodically in the trunk.

"Where to now, Ms. Harlow?" Paul asked as he climbed into the driver's seat.

Tapping a gloved finger against her lips, she looked at Kat. "What else do you need?"

"Something for Tristan."

Lizzy smiled. "Well, I can certainly help you with that."

Kat had been thinking about it all day. It had to be the right thing. Something he loved, something that he would cherish like she did the first edition of *The Mysterious Island* by Jules Verne he'd bought for her a few weeks before.

"I thought I might get him a map. Something old, or at least a reproduction of something old." A map was the most logical choice. He had confessed one night in bed that he was fascinated by cartography.

She'd known that first night he'd never before opened up to anyone the way he had to her. Talk about seduction of the heart, mind, and body...

"How did you know he liked maps?" Lizzy's question sliced through the delightful memories of Tristan's body wrapped around hers as he'd whispered about his dreams and secret joys.

"He...uh..." Words seemed to clog her throat, unable to get free. "He told me while we were Christmas tree shopping."

There. That sounded reasonable, didn't it?

"He did?" Lizzy was openly staring at her now.

Great. She kept forgetting she was supposed to know less about Tristan than she actually did.

"Yeah..." She tried to think fast. "I was telling him about how I liked Russian symphonies, and he said he liked old maps."

"I'm so glad you two are getting comfortable with each other." Lizzy seemed to relax. "Paul, take us to Standfords in Covent Garden."

"Yes, ma'am." The driver pulled out into traffic.

"What's Standfords?" Kat asked.

"A map store, among other things. They have quite the collection of rare map reproductions at good prices."

It sounded perfect. Lizzy had to be some sort of present genius.

The car pulled up in front of a store with bright red painted doors. STANDFORDS stood out in white block letters above the entrance. The windows were brightly decorated with maps, globes, and books about exotic lands like Morocco and Egypt.

Inside the store, Lizzy and Kat wandered the aisles and perused the shelves. Light walnut wood racks had dozens of maps draped over rungs, and small can lights illuminated the endless books along the walls.

Kat trailed a fingertip over each spine of the travel guides as she walked along, not seeing anything that seemed right. She froze when she reached a shelf with navigation tools on it. She found a rosewood box containing an antique brass compass with the year *1818* engraved on the brass cover.

"That's a lovely Brunton," Lizzy said, joining her by the shelf, her keen eyes roving over the compass's features.

"Do you think Tristan would like it?" She held her breath. Lizzy would tell her the truth, wouldn't she?

"Ah, yes, I think so." Lizzy smiled, but then she met Kat's gaze. "Are you and Tristan bonding? I know he can be a bit wild..."

That was an understatement. Tristan was untamable, a sex god that couldn't be ignored or resisted. Sleeping with him had pulled her apart cell by cell and put her back together. He'd *changed* her. Kat had fallen in love with him. *Wild* was definitely not the right word. He made her feel so many different things: new, exposed, and not herself.

"Tristan has been great. He's made me feel very welcome." Kat stroked her fingers over the brass surface of the compass.

He'd told her that he loved maps because they were like windows into the past, seeing how men and women viewed the world. A cultural memory frozen in time. Tristan had made maps seem beautiful, enchanting, and fascinating. But Kat wanted to give him something that would guide him. What good were maps if you didn't have a tool to read them? He needed to find his way in the world, make his own path separate from his father.

"I'm glad he's behaved himself," Lizzy said, but her tone was still serious. "He has a difficult time ahead. Between his father and his future title, he has so much to worry about, and I fear it's affected his relationships." She paused.

Kat held her breath until it seemed to singe her lungs with pain.

"What I mean is that he's not ready to settle down and date women. He's quite a charmer, and many decent women with good heads on their shoulders still vie for his attention, but he isn't serious about any of them. My son has left many broken hearts in his wake." When Lizzy met Kat's gaze, everything in Kat went still.

That sounds like a warning.

Tristan's mother knew about them. She *knew*...Kat tried not to panic, not to overreact or give herself away.

Lizzy placed a hand on Kat's wrist.

"It would be best if Clayton thought Tristan's heart-breaker tendencies wouldn't affect anyone he knew, especially someone he loves so very much." She gave Kat's now trembling hand a little pat and then tapped a finger on the compass. "You should get this for him. He doesn't have one, and I think he'll love it. You have an eye for beautiful things."

Kat glanced down at the compass. *God, please don't let Lizzy change her mind and tell Dad about us...* She didn't think Lizzy would risk upsetting Clayton, but she wasn't sure.

Collecting the compass, she headed to the cashier's desk, her legs shaking a little and her blood pounding in her ears. Everything would be fine; they wouldn't be discovered. She had to keep telling herself that and maybe she'd believe it.

Tonight they would open presents, and tomorrow was Christmas. Her *first* Christmas with her new family. It still hadn't sunk in. She was part of a bigger family now, one that included a stepmother and a stepbrother. The fact that she was sleeping with her future stepbrother...well, she couldn't let herself think about that right now.

As the man at the cash register wrapped up the compass, she noticed Lizzy talking on her phone. Her face was ashen, her grip on the phone white-knuckled.

"Please, Edward. Don't take him from me, not tonight," Lizzy pleaded, her head dropping and her eyes closed. Her fear turned to quiet rage as her lips thinned and her eyes narrowed. "You don't own me anymore. I made that clear when I left. You do not get to dictate what happens to me anymore." Lizzy's eyes opened again, and a steel fury burned in their depths. Then she disconnected the call, her anger flowing out of her as her shoulders dropped.

"Lizzy, is everything all right?" Kat collected her bag and joined Tristan's mother by the shop's entrance.

Slipping her phone back into her purse, Lizzy massaged her eyes and attempted to smile. "Tristan's father thinks he can stop me from marrying your father. He's threatened to keep my son away from me."

"But Tristan's not a child. It's not like you'd have a custody battle. He's twenty-five."

Lizzy shook her head. "It's complicated. Oh, I wish sometimes I'd never married Edward, but then"—she paused and a true smile lit her face—"I see my son, and I would endure that heartache all over again. That's why I named him Tristan."

"What do you mean?" Kat focused on Lizzy's eyes, hating the hurt she saw in the other woman's gaze.

"I didn't know when I married Edward that he was in love with someone else. I was..." Lizzy struggled for words. "A replacement for the woman he couldn't have. I found out a few months into our marriage, before I discovered I was pregnant. I was so happy in so many ways, but I knew I'd never win Edward's heart. Tristan was a child made from that grief. The name *Tristan* is French for *sadness*."

All around them the store was filled with customers, but Kat didn't notice them as she listened to Lizzy talk about something so intimate and personal.

"You named him?"

Lizzy nodded. "Edward wanted a family name, but I won that battle. I stayed with Edward as long as I could to give Tristan as normal a life as I could manage. That's what being a parent is. Making sacrifices to give the best to your child. It's instinct—it's love."

Kat's throat constricted and her eyes stung. Her mother hadn't felt that way about her. If she had...

She wouldn't have abandoned me and Dad.

"Kat?" Lizzy's hand clasped one of hers and squeezed. "I'm sorry if I upset you. I shouldn't have burdened you with these things."

"No—no, it's not that," Kat whispered. "I was just thinking how lucky Tristan is to have you. My mother..." A lump formed in her throat, choking anything else she might've said. But Lizzy was too perceptive.

"I imagine Tristan would feel the same way about you and your father. Clayton is wonderful, nothing like Edward." A rueful little smile curved her lips. "He's the kind of man I ought to have married. I'm glad to have the chance now." A delicate blush pinkened Lizzy's cheeks. "I hope Clayton and Tristan grow close someday. It would do Tristan some good to get to know a man who isn't driven by greed and ambition."

"Have you and Dad set a date for the wedding?" Kat asked.

"Not yet. I'm not sure I want a big wedding, so if your father doesn't want a big one either, we might be able to get married soon. We could even forgo the church and do a civil ceremony."

"You don't want a big wedding?"

Lizzy smiled softly. "No. Marrying your father is what matters. I don't care how it comes about, whether in a church and a white gown, or a simple wedding with just witnesses at the Mayor's Parlour."

Kat suddenly gasped when an idea struck her. "Lizzy, why don't you and Dad just get married today? You can, can't you?" In the short time she'd been around Lizzy, she had to admit the woman was good for her father. She laughed at his silly jokes, and the way she leaned in to him when they hugged and how he beamed down at her...There was true affection there, and her father had lost his tired, haggard look. Her dad was *happy*. What was the point in delaying?

Lizzy nibbled her lip, and then with a tentative smile, she looked at Kat. "Do you think your father would...? I mean, would he miss the fanfare of an official church wedding?"

Kat shook her head. "No, he wouldn't." She knew her dad well enough to know all that would matter was that he married Lizzy, and that Kat was there.

"Well, then, I suppose I ought to call him." With another girlish blush, Lizzy dialed Clayton.

Kat stepped toward the waiting car to give her some privacy, and she pulled out her own phone. After removing her gloves and stuffing them into her pockets, she texted Tristan.

Wedding is happening today. We're coming straight home.

Home. The word felt right now. Lizzy's town house was becoming home, just as Tristan already was.

Her phone vibrated seconds later, and she read the responding message.

Today?

Yes. She tapped her response. Was he going to be upset?

Very well.

Biting her lip, she typed again. *Are you mad?*

Rather than text her back, her phone rang and she answered instantly. "Hello?"

"Kat, as long as you stay with me, I don't care what our parents do. *You* are what matters to me."

She sighed, every ounce of tension in her suddenly evaporating.

"Now, come home so I can show you how much I've missed you." His soft chuckle turned her knees to jelly. How he had the power to do that, she'd never know.

"See you soon." She hung up and saw Lizzy watching her. Those fine lines of worry on her brow were deeper.

"Did you call Tristan?" Lizzy asked.

"Yeah, I thought I'd let him know..." Was she giving their secret away?

"Right," Lizzy said, her eyes still dark with a shadow of concern

She knows.

Lizzy really knows about Tristan and me.

Kat swallowed, faking a smile, and got into the car with Tristan's mother. Her father couldn't find out. Ever.

3

Tristan straightened his silver tie and took his place beside Clayton. As he studied Kat's father, Tristan had to admit the American cleaned up nicely. They both wore matching black tuxedos with silver waistcoats.

My stepfather. Tristan tried it out in his head. It didn't sound...terrible. The man was a nice fellow after all, and his mother adored him, which was what mattered most. Kat's father shifted restlessly and glanced at Tristan.

"I don't know why I'm so nervous." Clayton laughed.

"You'll do fine," Tristan assured him, but he too felt an odd stirring of nerves inside, as if he were the one getting married, not Clayton.

Kat's father nodded as though to steady his resolve. "I've never been more sure of anything in my life."

This marriage was going to be a good thing for both Clayton and Lizzy. Tristan wasn't blind, and he had noticed the changes in his mother since she had met Clayton. The happy animation of her features, the sunny glow of her smile, and the full laughter whenever Clayton teased her. It reminded Tristan of Kat, her laughter, her smiles.

Reaching out, he shook Clayton's hand.

"Thank you, Tristan. I can't tell you how much it means that you're supportive of our decision to marry. I know things are...rough with your father. I'm here for you, in whatever way you need me."

The genuine honesty in Clayton's face and voice filled Tristan with a strange cottony warmth. He blinked, a little startled by the sensation.

Before he and Clayton could say another word, the door to the Mayor's Parlour opened. The registrar, a short gray-haired man, smiled at them.

"The ladies are ready for you." The man nudged the door open more, letting Tristan and Clayton enter the room behind him.

The Mayor's Parlour was a warm, oak-paneled room in Town Hall, a fashionable Upper Street building that was home to the Registry Office. Vases filled with English wild-flowers covered the tables. The room had red leather armchairs, a couch, and burgundy carpets, along with the grand fireplace that was decorated with a coat of arms above the mantelpiece.

Next to the fireplace, his mother stood in a red knee-length dress with long sleeves and a scalloped bodice. It was an edgy fashion choice, to be sure, but he knew she was done being prim and proper. Her hair was down in soft romantic waves that glinted in the firelight, and the smile on her lips showed only a hint of nerves.

"Wow," Clayton whispered, a boyish grin on his face.

Tristan rolled his eyes. The man acted like a young lad with a schoolboy crush.

"Dad, you look great." Kat's voice pulled his focus away from Clayton, and Tristan's heart gave a little jolt, skipping a few beats.

Kat stood a few feet away from the fireplace in a

sapphire-colored cocktail dress. A thick white silk sash wound around her waist, and she wore white crystal-studded kitten-heeled shoes. Her skirts fluttered around the tops of her knees as she shifted on her feet. Her long brown hair had been pulled back from her face with a few jewel-studded butterfly pins.

He wanted to sink his hands into her hair and kiss her. The urge was so strong that he'd crossed the room and his hands were reaching for her before he'd even realized what he was doing. Catching himself just in time, he dropped his hands to her shoulders in a friendly, brotherly pat before he let go.

"You look wonderful, Kat," he said, forcing the huskiness out of his voice, as their parents were standing only a few feet away.

"Thank you. Your mother picked it out." Kat ruffled her dress while a sweet blush rose to her cheeks.

"Are we ready?" The registrar joined them by the fireplace.

Tristan moved to stand behind his mother, while Kat positioned herself behind her father.

She kept glancing his way, her gray eyes as soft as the down feathers of a mourning dove. When a little smile escaped onto her lips, it knocked him behind the knees.

The woman was his kryptonite. He couldn't resist her, *had* to have her.

Tristan was only vaguely aware of the wedding vows and the exchange of wedding bands. His entire body and mind were focused on Kat.

If he closed his eyes, he'd relive the moment he saw her in the glass coffin, the ruby gown so bright against her creamy skin. She'd been a fantasy, a lover ready to be awakened by his kiss.

When she'd impulsively kissed him in the pub that snowy night in Cambridge, he'd come undone and been reborn. He was done living the way he had, moving from lover to lover. None of it meant anything, and he was tired of feeling that way.

Kat's kiss had swept him off his feet like a rip current off the shore, and he didn't want to fight another second. Not when it meant they couldn't be together.

"I now pronounce you husband and wife." The registrar's declaration broke through Tristan's thoughts, and he blinked, suddenly remembering he was in the middle of his mother's wedding.

Lizzy was kissing Clayton, her lips curving into a smile while he held tightly on to her waist. They looked blissfully happy.

Tristan glanced back at Kat. Her eyes glinted with tears and she sniffed.

"Congratulations, Dad, Lizzy." Kat embraced them both when they broke apart.

"Thank you, Kat." Lizzy was teary-eyed, too, with happy tears.

"Are we ready to go home and eat Christmas Eve dinner?" Clayton clapped his hands together, which made Kat giggle, and her eyes met Tristan's.

"I have quite an appetite." Tristan smiled at her and then licked his lips. Another blush. She could obviously see he'd meant he was hungry for something else entirely.

"Good," Lizzy said. "Mrs. George will have baked up half the kitchen tonight."

Tristan caught Kat's waist when they fell into step behind their now-married parents.

"It's official, little sister," he murmured in her ear as he pulled her close. What he wouldn't give to drag her into the nearest closet and get his hands up her skirt so he could—

"*Stepsister*," she corrected in a breathless hiss so their parents wouldn't hear.

"Who knew this would feel *so bad?*" He squeezed her lightly, feeling the soft fabric of her dress crush beneath his fingers.

"Stop it, please. Not here," Kat begged him, but when her eyes met his, they were blazing with heated desire. She was as twisted up as he was and desperate to get a minute alone with him.

For a brief moment, as the four of them walked through Town Hall, the world seemed full of possibilities. Tristan thought his chest would burst with happiness.

They exited the building, and chaos erupted around them.

Cameras were everywhere, and a massive crowd of reporters were crushing in against them from all sides.

"Elizabeth Harlow, is it true you've just remarried? What does the Earl of Pembroke think about your new husband?" a man with the *Daily Mail* logo on his shirt shouted.

Clayton cursed and stumbled back, protecting Lizzy.

"Mum, the car is straight ahead!" Tristan shouted over the erupting madness of the press, while he covered Kat with his arms. She pressed in to his side and ducked her head.

"Out of the way!" Clayton bellowed, and started shoving men out of his path to the waiting car.

"Mr. Kingsley, is this your new girlfriend? Is she your stepsister?"

Another camera flash, then lights dotted his vision, and he clutched Kat to him, trying to half carry her to the car.

"Tristan!" Kat cried out when someone grabbed her arm, attempting to tug her from Tristan's hold.

Before he could think it through, Tristan reacted and swung a fist, landing a blow on a man's jaw.

The reporter let go of Kat's arm.

"That bugger punched me!" the reporter screeched, but Tristan didn't care as he got Kat and his mother into the car.

Their parents climbed into the middle seat and he and Kat got into the backseat behind them.

"Tristan, you didn't hit him, did you?" Lizzy glanced out the car windows at the flock of reporters still taking photos.

He wrapped an arm around Kat's shoulders and pressed a kiss to her temple. His body was flooded with adrenaline and rage. Tristan was sick of the paps getting in his face, frightening the people he cared about. He would do anything to protect Kat, anything because she meant *everything*.

"Lizzy." Clayton's voice pulled Tristan's attention to the front. Kat's father was half turned around in his seat, staring at them.

"Yes, dear?" Lizzy's nervous gaze darted between her husband and Tristan.

"That reporter said something about Kat and Tristan...*dating*?"

Lizzy swallowed, then laughed. "Oh—that's ridiculous, dear."

Their car turned the corner, leaving the reporters behind, but Tristan cursed as a bus pulled up alongside them. A large ad was on its side. An ad he recognized with dread. Prince Charming kissing Snow White.

"What in the *hell*?" Clayton's eyes widened as he took in the ad, then narrowed to slits as he turned to stare at Lizzy.

Tristan swallowed hard. This was it. They'd been outed before he was ready. A knot tightened in his stomach as he struggled to come up with a new plan. There was no way Kat's father would buy the story they'd told his mother this morning.

"Kat, why are you kissing Tristan on a bus ad?"

"Dad—" Kat tried to pull away from Tristan, but he wouldn't let her go. It was all going to come out and there was no stopping it.

He rubbed the back of his neck as heat flooded his face.

Anxiety spiraled inside him, but a secret part of him was relieved to have things out in the open.

"Clayton, Kat and I *are* dating."

Kat sucked in a harsh breath and went rigid against his side. She was going to be furious with him.

"What? You're joking." Clayton's brows lowered and his lips pursed into an angry line.

"Dad—" Kat's lips quivered, and Tristan felt her entire body quake.

"We've been seeing each other for a few weeks, since Cambridge. I have only honorable intentions toward her." He almost couldn't believe how strong his voice came out, when everything inside him was flipping on its head. But he meant it; he wanted to date Kat for as long as he could. He didn't want to think about the future when things could change.

The harsh laugh sounded more like a snarl when it escaped Clayton's lips. "Honorable? Tristan, your mother told me all about you. Your womanizing, the affairs, the scandals. I know you're young and reckless, but that doesn't mean you can take my daughter for another notch in your bedpost."

"It isn't like that," Tristan argued, his frustration rolling through him hard enough that he had to clench his fists.

"Dad, you have to let me explain." Kat leaned forward in her seat, but Clayton glowered at her. Her shocked inhalation made Tristan's heart clench.

"I thought you had better sense than that, Katherine. Your studies are crucial. Now is not the time to jeopardize your future by getting distracted by someone like him. He'll drop you and move on to someone else in a matter of days. He has a reputation, Kat. I warned you about him," Clayton growled.

Tristan tried to pull Kat back into the safety of his arms.

"Clayton." Lizzy's voice was soft, wounded. "He's my son..."

Tristan was used to his reputation causing him some discomfort socially, the disapproving looks, the whispers, the articles, but none of that had hurt him like this. Clayton's open anger cut deep.

"If anything, it's my fault, not hers," Tristan said, meeting his mother's eyes. "From the moment I met Kat, I wanted her. Don't blame her for any of this." He turned his gaze back to Clayton, ready for battle.

"At least you have enough sense to accept responsibility. But it's over. Do you understand?" Clayton's imperious declaration was all too familiar.

It was like fighting with his father all over again. He wasn't going to let another man tell him what to do, especially one with no hold over him.

Tristan's lips parted, another protest ready, but Kat spoke up first.

"Dad, you don't get to dictate my life. I'm nineteen. I'm an adult, and my life is all my own. You can accept my choices or not, but you can't control me."

"I can, Katherine. You're still my daughter, and I don't want you getting hurt." The anger that had flared so hot in Clayton's eyes lessened slightly, as though the man was seeing Kat differently for the first time in his life.

"So it's your way or the highway, is that it?" Kat asked.

Tristan sensed she was on the verge of losing her nerve because her hands were trembling when he covered them with his.

"Why don't we wait until we return home to talk about this," Tristan suggested. His heart thudded hard in his chest, and he was strangely nervous. He'd never cared about any woman like this before. Seeing her quarrel with her father because of him and his selfish need to have her...He felt...very *guilty*, because he had no intention of giving Kat up.

"Tristan's right." His mother touched Clayton's shoulder, and while he didn't pull away, he frowned.

"Did you know about this?" Accusation layered his tone, and the look of hurt in Lizzy's eyes shot a bolt of pain through Tristan's chest.

Kat had been right. This would tear their parents apart.

"I—"

"She didn't know." Tristan cut his mother off. "If you have a problem with my relationship with your daughter, you will take it out on me, not Mum. Is that clear?" He met Clayton's eyes with a cold stare. This wouldn't be the first time he'd stood between a cruel bastard and his mother. As soon as he was old enough to argue, he'd put himself between his father and Lizzy time and again, trying his best to protect her.

The fire in Clayton's eyes melted away and his frown faded. "I'm not upset with Lizzy. I'm just upset. I'd never do anything to hurt your mother."

A tender touch brushed Tristan's thigh, and he glanced down to see Kat's hand there. When he looked her way, she was nibbling her lip in concern as she met his eyes. He took her hand and covered it with his own, squeezing gently.

"Let's just talk about this when we get home," Kat said, her gaze darting between him and her father.

The occupants of the car settled into an uncomfortable silence for the rest of their journey. Paul, the driver, kept his gaze decidedly focused on the road ahead, as though he was determined to become invisible.

Tristan's blood pounded like distant war drums against his temples, and he failed miserably at convincing himself that this wouldn't end badly.

When Paul stopped in front of the house, Lizzy and Kat's father got out first. They moved up the icy walkway in a cold silence. When the butler opened the door for them, his pleasant expression faded as he saw their expressions. Tristan gave him a small, forced smile as he was the last to come inside.

"Katherine, I want a word with you *alone*." Clayton gripped her arm firmly, escorting her to the library, where he closed the doors, leaving Tristan and his mother standing in the foyer.

Tristan dropped his head back and stared at the ceiling, trying to breathe.

His mother reached for his hand. "Tristan, how long have you and Kat been...?"

Thrusting his hands into his pockets to avoid his mother's touch, Tristan paced the length of the foyer a few times before he slowed to a stop. The murmur of voices in the library was too soft and muffled by the thick wooden doors.

"We met at Cambridge. Before Christmas break. I've been seeing her on and off." He scraped a hand over his jaw, unable to stop moving, stop pacing, as restlessness rolled through him. He knew it wouldn't go away until Kat was in his arms again.

His mother's lips parted and she exhaled before speaking, her voice low and soft. "On and off?"

He shrugged and finally faced her. "Yes. We had a few fits and starts at first. She didn't like seeing me in the rags with Brianna, and when we found out we were to be stepsiblings, she broke it off then, too. She was afraid of this. She warned me it would break you and Clayton up."

At this, his mother laughed, a quiet, slightly strained sound. "Well, it's not how I imagined our wedding day, or our first Christmas Eve, but it certainly won't break us up."

"I'm not sure if I believe that, Mum. Clayton seems furious." His eyes fixed on the closed library door. *What is he saying to her?* Was he talking her into breaking up with him again? She promised she wouldn't, not as long as they both wanted this. And he still did. More than ever before.

His mother walked in between him and the library door, catching his attention again.

"He couldn't be more different from your father. He talks to me. We don't fight, not like your father and I did. It doesn't mean we don't get upset sometimes, but this won't end our relationship. When two people are in love, they make it work."

"You'd do anything to be with them." Tristan thought of how hard it had been to be without Kat for even a few days. He'd done everything he could to convince her they could make this work.

"Yes, exactly," his mother agreed.

Again, Tristan's focus turned to the library.

"They need time to talk, Tristan. Go make yourself useful and hang stockings above the beds. I haven't done that yet. Then go ask Mrs. George how our pudding fairs this year."

She was deliberately trying to keep him busy and distracted, but Mum was right. He couldn't wear a path into the carpets with his pacing.

With one last glance at the library door, he stalked off to do as his mother suggested. Kat would find him when they were done. He planned to hold her to her promise that she wouldn't walk away. Tristan had to, because he couldn't bear to lose her again.

❧ 4 ❧

Kat stood in front of the library windows beneath the stained-glass Saint George as he slayed the green dragon. These were the windows Tristan had seen as a child, the ones that had moved him to such strong emotions.

How far they'd both come since the night they'd met and kissed at the Pickerel Inn pub.

Kat longed for that moment so many days ago, when the snow was falling outside, along with the muted sounds of pubgoers chatting nearby, the warmth of Tristan's body close to hers as they whispered, teased, and flirted. She wanted to trap that moment in time, bottle it and save it.

She was ready to battle her father for the one thing in her life she didn't want to give up: Tristan.

She clutched her little black purse and shifted restlessly in the low heels she wore. Kat wanted to get out of the fancy dress and back into her warm jeans and sweater. She felt off-balance, and that was the last thing she needed right now.

"Kat, what were you *thinking?*" Her father stood ten feet

away, leaning back against a reading table. The old weariness she'd grown used to over the last few years had returned.

It's my fault. Mine. Because I want Tristan.

"Dad…" Words failed her. What she and Tristan shared couldn't be easily described. It spread outward from her like a beacon from a lighthouse, through wind and rain, shining ever onward.

"You know what sort of man he is, don't you? He's wild, Kat. Reckless. He's not someone you would settle down with."

Tristan was wild and reckless, but he was also sweet, compassionate, and so damn sexy when it came to her, she couldn't find fault with anything he'd done. He'd only ever been perfect.

"He's not like that. Well, part of him is, but he's so much *more*." She stepped closer to her father, still holding tight to her purse.

"Honey, you can't date him. Pick *anyone* but him." She recognized that tone. It was his business voice, calm, almost cold.

He wasn't going to budge on his opinion of Tristan.

But neither was she.

All along Tristan had been pushing her to see what lay between them. Not just the sparks in bed, but everything else. She wasn't going to let go of him, not until things were done. So far things were better than ever, hotter than ever. If her father was allowed his chance at happiness in life, then so was she.

Taking in a steadying breath, Kat met her father's fierce gaze.

"I care about him, Dad. *A lot*. What we have…it's amazing. It's like what you and Lizzy—"

"Don't compare yourself to me and Lizzy." He waved a hand in the air, dismissing her defense. "We're both divorced, we've been through heartache, and we know what we're looking for in life. You're a child, Kat. You don't know the first thing about love or relationships. He'll still be here even after you stop dating. He'll be a part of this family, and you'll have to face him. Can you do that after he breaks your heart?"

It wasn't something she wanted to think about, the idea of Tristan breaking her heart, but it was a very real possibility he would do just that.

It was too late. She'd fallen for him, and walking away now would hurt just as much. What did it matter when something happened, if it was inevitable? She wanted to enjoy every minute of it until it was over.

"It's too late, Dad. I...I love him." The word came out in a hushed whisper, but her lips curled into a smile. Saying it out loud filled her with a joy that made the world glow and her heart race. She was completely, totally in love with Tristan. She'd feared loving him because she knew she'd lose him. Right now she wanted to fight for him and there was no turning back. She couldn't stop loving him just to please her father and she didn't want to. She was jumping off a cliff and free-falling. It was scary and exhilarating.

Her dad's bitter laugh cut her deep. "Love? Honey, what you're feeling is infatuation. It rarely lasts. I learned that the hard way with your mother. Tristan's a handsome young man, and you're just swept up in the moment. What you feel for him isn't real. Someday, when you're older and not so wide-eyed and innocent, you'll meet the real love of your life." There was a bite to his tone that stung, and Kat flinched.

How could he so casually dismiss feelings that went bone deep inside her? How could he possibly know what *she* felt wasn't real? Just because she was young didn't mean it was any less *real*. What she'd felt for Tristan that first night, that spark of lightning, a recognition of two souls connected, hadn't diminished in the following weeks, but had grown steadily stronger.

"Dad, if I fall for someone, that's my business, my life. I'm entitled to make my own decisions."

"And your own mistakes? Kat, honey, I'm trying to keep you from getting hurt." Clayton uncrossed his arms and pushed away from the table he'd been leaning against.

"Yes. My own mistakes. Why can't you just give Tristan a chance?"

"No."

"But—"

"No. You will not date that boy while under this roof. Do you understand?"

She didn't recognize the man standing in front of her. He wasn't her father, at least not the one she knew.

Tears stung her eyes and fury battled with despair. This wasn't up to *him*. He didn't have a right to dictate her life. He'd drawn a line in the sand and given her an ultimatum. There was only one choice left.

"If you're going to be like that, I'm going back to Cambridge." She spun and shoved the library door open.

"Kat, honey, wait—"

Slam! She purposely let the door crash into the frame. She didn't want to see him again, not until he was being reasonable.

Lizzy appeared at the kitchen door, her brows knitted in consternation, but she didn't say anything as Kat raced upstairs. That was one of the many things she liked about Tristan's mother. She didn't try to pry or insert herself into Kat's business. When the library door opened and her father rushed out, Kat had just reached the top of the stairs.

"Kat, I'm not done talking to you. Get back down here." He was scowling, one shoe tapping.

"I'm done talking, Dad." She turned away and walked to her room.

When she flung the door open, she halted at the sight of Tristan leaning over her bed, a red and gold brocade stocking in one hand and a hammer in the other. A nail hung from his lips, as if he seemed to be debating where to put it.

"What are you doing?" she asked, her chest rising and falling heavily as she sought to regain her breath. Fighting with her dad had left her anxious and strung out. Her arms shook and her knees threatened to buckle. All she wanted to do was collapse on her bed and cry. But she wasn't a child. She had to hold herself together.

Tristan set the hammer, nail, and stocking down and walked over to her. "It's an English tradition...We hang the stockings over the bed, not the fireplace."

She lifted her head, met his gaze, and the floodgates broke. Kat threw herself against him, hugging him tight and burying her face against his chest.

He wrapped his arms around her back and waist, resting his chin on top of her head. The embrace, all-encompassing and warm, made the agony in her heart ease a little.

"I'm so sorry, darling. What can I do?" His deep voice rumbled against her ear.

"Just hold me," she whispered. He grounded her, keeping her from drifting away on the vast flowing river of pain.

Dad and I have never fought like that. Never.

What if he didn't forgive her? What if it destroyed her father's relationship with Lizzy? What if—

"Hey..." Tristan threaded his fingers through her hair and gently massaged her scalp. "Don't think so hard. Just breathe."

She forced deep, shaking breaths into her lungs, and like magic, that simple act of breathing made some of her panic dissipate, even though she couldn't stop trembling.

She pulled back so she could see Tristan's face. His dark hair fell across his eyes, reminding her of the way he'd looked when they'd made love back at Fox Hill.

A master of her pleasure, he'd made the world explode around them in invisible sparks. That night had lit a fire that had only grown in passing days. He'd held her in his arms and she'd known how much he cared for her. She didn't want to be around anyone but him right now. He was the only one who understood her and what she was feeling.

"Can you take me somewhere? I need to leave. My dad and I..."

"Where do you want to go?" He rubbed his palms up and down her back, and she leaned in again, resting her cheek against his chest above his heart.

"Could we go back to Cambridge? I don't really have anywhere else to go."

"What about Fox Hill?" he suggested. "It would be just you and me. No one else...except for the servants."

She gave a watery giggle. "Why is it that talking to you sometimes sounds so ridiculous? Just us and the servants, darling," she teased in an attempt to imitate his accent.

"You truly want to leave?" He brushed a lock of hair back from her face so tenderly her heart turned over.

"Let's do it. Let's go right now." Rolling up on her tiptoes, she kissed his chin, then his lips, and relished watching his lashes fan up and down as he gave in to her kiss.

His fingertips dug into her back as though he was on the verge of gripping her hard, but he pulled away, licked his lips, and breathed out slowly.

"Pack a bag and change. I'll be back soon. If I stay here right now, you won't leave your bed for a few hours. And your father might shoot me." His wry chuckle didn't erase the sting of the truth to their situation.

Tristan was right. Space would do them both some good.

I just need some time to think, that's all. So does my dad. He'll come around. He has to.

With another brush of lips, Tristan left her alone to pack.

Fifteen minutes later she was changed and carrying her duffle bag down the stairs. Tristan was a few feet ahead of her, his own leather travel bag slung over his shoulder.

They were almost to the door when her father strode out to meet them. His lips were in a grim line and his hands were shoved deep into his pockets. Lizzy joined them, her hands clasped tensely together, as though she was unsure of what to do.

The foyer was thick with tension. Kat felt like the four of them were facing off.

"Don't leave," her father said. He kept his eyes on her and ignored Tristan.

"Only if you change your mind." Kat wasn't going to back down. Not on something this important.

"No. I've told you how I feel, and that hasn't changed."

Her throat stung as she fought off a sob. "Ok-kay. Then we're leaving until you do." Without looking at her dad again, she reached for Tristan's hand, and they walked past their parents to the entrance.

"Kat, please..." It was the last thing she heard before Tristan shut the door behind them.

5

Kat had chosen him over her father? Conflicting emotions spiraled through him: elation, worry, pride, regret. The only person she had left to call family in this world, and she'd walked away from the man for him. Would he have done the same if he'd been forced to? Leave his mother like that to keep Kat in his life? The idea of being without her...He repressed a shudder.

Kat truly belonged to him, for however long he could keep her.

"I'm sorry," he whispered, holding her hands tight in his. "You shouldn't have to choose."

I'm a bloody bastard for being happy she chose me. Guilt turned his insides to fire, and he forced the sickening sensation down as deep as he could. It was almost Christmas, and he and Kat were together, just as he'd wanted.

She wiped her face with her free hand and laughed, but the sound was full of pain. "Well, I had to. Let's go."

He put the bags in the trunk and glanced back at his mother's town house.

I'm sorry, Mum.

Tristan hated leaving her behind, but she had Clayton now, and Kat needed him more. Everything that had happened to her was because she couldn't stay away from him and he couldn't keep his hands off her.

Tristan wasn't sure how long they drove in silence before he glanced at Kat. She'd stared at her phone a few times when it had buzzed and he'd seen the name "Dad" on her screen before she silenced it. Now she was reclined back in her seat with her eyes closed. Her features were a little relaxed, and she looked peaceful in her sleep. He blew out a breath, and some of the tension in his muscles eased.

I finally have what I want. Kat all to myself. She'd left her father to be with him, for what…hot sex? They'd both sacrificed too much to stay together. All he could think about was how lucky he was that Kat saw something in him worth fighting for. She made him feel like a damned hero when she gazed up at him with those eyes so full of intensity and a promise of things he hadn't known he wanted until he'd met her.

She was a future, a future he wanted to claim as his, but he knew it wasn't something he would be allowed to keep. That day in Kew Gardens they'd both acknowledged that he was expected to marry someone groomed to be a countess. Someone his father approved of. But he didn't want to dwell on the future he knew his father wanted for him.

I can cling to this fantasy for just a little while longer, can't I?

About two hours later, they were climbing the front steps of Fox Hill. The butler, Mr. Whitney, was there to greet them.

"Whitney, this is Kat Roberts. She's my…er…" *Stepsister…girlfriend…*

"Friend," Kat interjected, saving him.

"Welcome, Ms. Roberts. Good evening, Mr. Kingsley."

The butler shouldered Kat's duffle and held the door open to allow them in.

Rubbing her arms, Kat allowed her gaze to rove over the entryway of the house.

"What is it?" Tristan curled an arm around her, offering warmth.

When she turned her face toward his, she was smiling. It was a smile of genuine delight. "I *love* this house. It's so beautiful."

"So do I." He led her inside, eager to show her more. She'd stayed here before, after the party he'd held following the end of the year's exams, but they'd both been more focused on ripping each other's clothes off than on a tour.

"So this was where you spent a lot of time with your mother?"

"Yes, quite often. Kew Gardens was our refuge in London, but Fox Hill was truly hers. My father rarely set foot in this place."

They walked farther into the house, and he tried to see everything through her eyes. The rich reds of the walls and the warmth of the wood paneling. The scent of books from the library, the creak and sighs of the house settling into place as a wind from outside rushed over the brick facade. Rows of portraits of ancestors, even one of him by the top of the stairs. Her eyes focused on that painting. She wrinkled her nose, as if deep in thought.

"What are you thinking?" Tristan was always fascinated by her mind and the thoughts that flashed through it.

"When I came here before, I didn't notice that painting. I was hurting so much for having sent you away, and when I showed up for the party, I walked right past it." She cocked her head slightly to one side, really studying the picture. "I like it. You look like you know just who you are."

Inside the frame, his oil counterpart stood tall and proud,

chin raised, eyes clear and intense. He was wearing a blue three-piece suit and standing beside a marble fireplace. The background was dark, as if to create an illusion that he was a dark god of the underworld stepping out of his domain into the light. He'd always thought the painting was too grim, too brooding, but now he was seeing it in a different way.

There was a look of purpose in his eyes and a determined set to his chin, as though he knew just what he wanted to do with his life. Had being with Kat made him see things in a new light? He'd never embraced his destiny as the future Earl of Pembroke. Yet talking about his plans for the estate with Kat when they were alone made him want to be a good man, and a good earl. A better man than his father. Now he had a real desire to enact the plans he and Carter had dreamed up. He had been too afraid to push for change until Kat had reminded him he was strong. He could take control of his life again and run the estate to benefit everyone, not just the family's pocketbook. And he had Kat to thank for it.

"You really like it?" he asked.

She nodded seriously. "It suits you. Reminds me of the night I first saw you." With an impish twinkle in her eyes, Kat nudged him with an elbow. "What did you think when you first saw me?"

He curled an arm around her waist and stroked her hair back from her face as he summoned his memories of that night. "I thought I was dreaming. Everything around you was like a blurry scene from a Monet and you were there, like a woman out of a Sargent painting, real, vivid laughter in your eyes and your heart on your sleeve when you opened up to me at the bar. It was like I'd taken a deep breath for the first time in years."

The tiny pupils in her eyes grew as she blinked. "That's really what you thought?" Kat's lips twitched as though she was tempted to smile but was a little afraid of showing how much she wanted to.

"That was only the beginning. Everything now is so much more intense."

Finally, she smiled. "It's that way for me, too."

For a moment neither of them said anything. They just held on to each other, foreheads pressed together, eyes closed, sharing breath and warmth.

Tristan broke the contact first because he wanted to show her more of the house. Fox Hill was full of memories for him, more often good than bad.

"Let me show you the rest." He nodded at the hall.

Mr. Whitney emerged, in that uncanny way a good butler could, to take their coats and put them away in the closet.

"Whitney, we'll be around the house a bit. Is there anything to eat in the kitchen for later?"

The butler nodded. "Mrs. March left out some cookies she was planning to frost, and there's homemade cocoa in the tin by the teapot. If you don't mind, I'll pop down to town for a few hours to take care of a few things before this evening." Then Mr. Whitney made himself scarce, which was good because Tristan wanted to take Kat straight to bed.

"Cookies? Oh, Tristan, I haven't frosted cookies since I was a kid. Can we?" Kat's bright smile banished away the lingering ghosts of his worries.

"We just arrived home and rather than"—he made a subtle hand gesture that earned him a sweet blush—"you want to frost cookies?" He didn't know whether to be irritated or amused at her ability to string him out. He wanted to drag her to bed and fuck her bloody brains out.

"Yes. Cookies. Then..." She mimicked the gesture with her hands, a wicked smile that suited her too well hovering on her lips. "Wouldn't you like to see what interesting things we can do with frosting?" She made a deliberate show of licking her lips.

And just like that, his cock was punching at the front of his jeans and his blood heated. He reached out to grip her waist with his hands and tug her close to whisper, "Fine. I'll agree to the terms. Cookies, then you in my bed wearing nothing and on your hands and knees like a good little girl, because I have an entire Christmas list of bad, very bad things I want to do to you."

This time her face turned beet-red and her lips parted.

"How bad?" she asked in a breathless whisper.

"So bad, I'll get a stocking full of coal for the next century." His fingers tightened on her hips and he kissed the shell of her ear while rubbing his erection against her stomach.

Another panting breath, and her body quivered in his hold.

Now *he* wanted to be the one who tortured her after all the times she'd nearly killed him with her sweet sensuality. He knew after years of seduction when a woman was heavily aroused. Kat's eyes were slightly dilated and her breath came out in shallow pants. "How about those cookies?" He rotated her body so she was facing the direction that would take them to the kitchen, and he took her arm in his as they walked together. She was glaring at him, but there wasn't any real anger there.

"You got me all revved up on purpose, didn't you." It wasn't a question.

"Tit for tat, darling. I never said I play fair." Tristan gave her arse a rather rough little pat before he crossed the kitchen to fetch the teapot. When he turned back around, she was staring at him, more specifically staring at his lower body.

"What is it?" he asked.

"Hmm?" she replied as though still distracted. "Oh, sorry, I was just looking at your ass and picturing my hands digging into it while you're on top of me...*inside* me." She bit her bottom lip to hide a smile.

"Little minx. You realize, I'm this close..." He held up his hand and pinched his thumb and forefinger in the air, leaving only half an inch between them.

She was teasing him sexually, and it was driving him wild, not just physically. He'd never really had a woman be this playful about sex. Sure, there had been lots of woman who'd played the game with him, the coy smiles, the questing palms in dark corners of clubs, the hand jobs in the bathrooms of expensive restaurants...but this...with Kat? It was different. It was more exciting, more intense, more rewarding than anything else had been with those other women.

"Why don't you make us the cocoa and I'll find the frosting and the cookies." Kat changed the subject just when he'd decided to hell with it. The look she sent him, eyes alight with mischief, as though she'd known how hard he was from her teasing, was too damned adorable.

Tristan stared at her as he held the teapot in one hand. Adorable? He'd never used the word before with a woman, but he kept using it with Kat. She located the cookies in a red and white Christmas tin and then dug around in the cupboards for plates. Tristan knew he wasn't going to cut the cookies and cocoa out of their plans, so he filled the kettle and twisted the knobs on the stovetop to heat the water.

Kat had placed all the cookies on plates and was digging through the drawers until, with a little "aha!" she pulled out a pair of small butter knives.

"Where do you suppose she put the jar of frosting?" she asked, her eyes darting around the kitchen.

With a little chuckle, Tristan shook his head at her. "You

think any cook who works for my mother would use premade frosting? Good Lord, Kat. We're the aristocracy, not common folk." He raised his chin in a mock-haughty manner, but at the look on her face, as though she half believed him, he burst out laughing.

"Well, seriously though, darling. Mrs. March would never use canned frosting. She's an excellent cook and takes pride in her work."

"Hmm." Kat pursed her lips and pulled out her phone, typing on it.

"What on earth are you doing?" He walked over to her and peered down at her screen.

This time she laughed. "I'm Googling frosting."

"Googling?" He almost choked on the word. "You're trusting the fate of Mrs. March's Christmas cookies to a search engine?" He looked up at the ceiling, sighing dramatically, but Kat nudged him hard in the ribs with her elbow.

"Google has never failed me before." She snickered at some private joke and then held up her screen. "Homemade frosting recipe using powdered sugar. All we need is buttermilk, a block of cream cheese, and powdered sugar."

Tristan squeezed Kat's waist lightly before he let her go, and then they both dug through the fridge and cabinets until they found the ingredients. As it turned out, creating frosting from scratch was a sticky business. Once it was all done and the cookies were frosted, Kat's russet-brown hair was lightly dusted with the sugary powder, and he had handprint-shaped stains on his jeans from where he'd patted his hands without thinking.

"God, we've made a mess!" Kat glanced at the smattering of bowls and the plates covered in bits of discarded frosting.

"Mrs. March will be furious," he agreed.

With one arched brow, Kat stared at him. "Oh no, Mr.

Future Earl, you're doing the dishes with me. I'm not leaving poor Mrs. March to deal with all of this when she gets back."

Doing his best, he followed Kat's lead on the dishes, but he quickly discovered that he did not like to wash things in the sink. The entire time she was giggling and trying to hide it, as though his inability to use a scrub brush was hilarious.

"You know I'm going to make you pay for this. In bed. With lots of sex." He winked at her. There were a hundred ways he wanted to punish his little Kitty-Kat, and he had a drawer full of toys in his bedroom to use on her.

"Everyone should know how to clean dishes. Even aristocrats."

Her laughter, which followed, was musical, and the sweet sound of it punched him in the gut. His heart gave a strange rush of quick beats before it calmed again. Lord, she was beautiful, and it wasn't just her killer curves, but the way a twinkle brightened her gray eyes and how her smile made her face light up.

As Kat set the last dish into the dishwasher, Tristan tossed the brush into the sink and groaned. "Tell me we're done with this." He waved a hand at the counter.

She studied the kitchen; it looked almost as spotless as when they had entered. "I think so. What do you want to do next?" Kat wiped her hands dry on a towel and turned to face him.

Tristan cocked a brow. "I seem to remember someone promising to be in my bed, naked, on hands and knees...Ring any bells?" he teased.

"Right." Kat flushed and glanced down, a tad bashful.

He curled his arms around her back, holding her close. "What's this? Getting shy on me? I'm afraid we can't have that." He met her gaze. "Why don't we play a game of billiards?" That sounded innocent enough. She wouldn't know until it was too late that he intended to break down some of those modesty barriers in a creative way.

"Pool? I'd like that. I'm not very good, but I can play." She grinned.

"Excellent." He was damned good at pool and had a very good idea of how to strip his little American stepsister out of all those pesky clothes she didn't need.

Merry Christmas to me...

6

Tristan took Kat to the large entertainment room on the first floor. It had once been his grandfather's cigar and brandy room, but had since been converted to a sort of "man cave," with a billiard table, leather couches, and a sixty-five-inch flat-screen on one wall. The low-hanging lamps above the billiard table illuminated the green felt when Tristan turned on the lights.

"Select a few cues. I'll pour us some brandy." He headed to the liquor cabinet by the TV and poured two glasses before coming back to her.

A pair of cues rested on the felt and Kat was positioning the balls inside the wooden triangle.

"Solids or stripes?" she asked as she tucked the last ball inside with the others.

"Solids." He set the white ball down on the black dot and lifted his cue. "But let's make it interesting."

"Okay." Kat carefully extracted the wooden triangle and set it back on the rack by the extra cues. "Like a wager on who wins?"

"Something like that. How about"—Tristan leaned over

the table, cue ready for his shot—"whoever sinks their ball in a pocket gets to pick an item of clothing to remove from the other person."

Kat's eyes glinted as she regarded him silently for a long moment. "One question. Do socks count as two items or the pair as one?"

Chuckling, Tristan smacked the white ball hard and it knocked all the other balls into a wild disarray on the table.

"Definitely one." He wanted to get her naked as fast as he could.

"My turn." Kat bumped him away from the table with her hip and prepared for her shot. Rather than watch her take her turn, he stared at her delectable arse, wishing it was bare so he could stroke the soft skin.

"Yes!" Kat whooped and straightened, pointing her cue at a striped ball that had just dropped into a corner pocket. "Take off your shirt." She nudged him with her pole. "That's right, take it off." She encouraged him with a sultry little laugh that shocked him with a bolt of desire.

He was going to get her for that. Definitely. He unbuttoned his shirt and draped it over the back of the couch.

"My turn." He sank the next hit, three solids going into pockets and one striped.

"You hit one of mine in and that means you get to take something else off," Kat announced, and pointed at his boots. "Pairs as one, just like the socks."

Without a complaint, he toed off his boots. "Fine. Boots off. Now you get to take something off." He walked around her in a slow circle, studying her jeans, her sweater, and the little black boots she wore. "Boots... socks...sweater." He crossed his arms and leaned back against the billiard table while he waited for her to do as he asked.

Muttering adorable curses under her breath, Kat tugged

off her boots and socks and then lifted her sweater up and off, dropping it on the couch next to his shirt.

Fuck. He'd been hoping she'd have nothing but a bra on underneath. Instead, she was wearing a black T-shirt that hugged her breasts. So much for his big win.

Then she padded around him on her little bare feet and studied the current lay of the balls on the table before picking her position. Right when she started to take her shot, he lifted the end of his cue and caressed it lightly along the inside of her right leg. With a little startled yelp, she knocked the balls in a dozen directions, but without enough force to send them toward the pockets.

She spun on him, furious. "Why, you cheating—"

Tristan silenced her by covering her mouth with his. He used his lips and tongue, sensually teasing her roughly, reminding her that he was in control of this little game and that she would be begging for him in seconds.

Kat curled her arms around his neck, kissing him back, her mouth hungry, desperate, echoing what he was feeling.

"Bloody hell, woman. Forget the game," he growled, and lifted her up, dropping her on her arse on the edge of the pool table.

The frantic shedding of clothes had them both laughing and pausing briefly to steal kisses before he had his pants around his ankles and Kat completely bare. The lamplight played upon her skin, creating soft shadows in the curves of her body, the curves he wanted to spend hours worshipping with his mouth. She shivered and gazed up at him as he gently but firmly pressed her to lie flat on the table. A few billiard balls rolled away as she settled onto the surface, and her lips parted as she drew in a shaky breath.

"Tristan, you're so...perfect." Her cheeks reddened, and she didn't say anything else but smiled up at him.

In that moment he would have conquered the world for

her. Done anything she'd asked. He wanted to shout from the rooftops, crow like a young lad with triumph, and he couldn't even say why. There was just a strange warmth in his chest that made him feel a tad light-headed, almost giddy.

Nudging her legs apart, he pulled her to the edge of the table and, watching her eyes, began to penetrate her slowly, entering inch by inch as she stared back at him. Invisible strands seemed to weave their bodies together, connecting them completely. He rocked slowly, breathing hard as he struggled to be gentle at first. Kat held up one hand, reaching for him, and he understood what she wanted. Bending over her, he covered her body with his and kissed her while he fucked her. It felt different somehow. Just the two of them at Fox Hill, able to be together without worrying that one or both of their parents would stumble in on them by accident.

"You feel like fucking heaven," he whispered against her throat.

Her body was hot and tight around his, drawing him deeper and deeper into her with each thrusting move. It was glorious, this wild rush of pleasure. He poured himself into her with every kiss, every teasing touch of his fingers over the curves of her hips and breasts. She was incredible, arching up, throwing her head back...He was lost in the way the light rippled along the tangle of her hair over the green felt. Her nails dug into his back, and she gasped his name over and over again like a fervent prayer.

There was no containing the explosion within him at the sound of his name as she burned up in a blaze of passion while she climaxed. His body tensed. Everything in him seemed to drive straight to his cock, and his blood roared against his eardrums. He shouted out her name as he let go and came inside her. She took everything in that moment, even his soul, and he didn't want it to end, the rippling pleasure of her body around his, the twitching of every muscle in his legs as he struggled to stay on his feet.

There weren't words for either of them for several seconds. He propped himself up and brushed the back of his knuckles over her cheek, smiling.

"We should..." Her voice was broken by her breathing. "Play pool again soon."

"I agree." He chuckled.

It was a long while later when they'd finally left the billiard room and were properly dressed again. He held her hand as they walked down the hall.

"Are you going to show me the rest of the house?" She gave his hand a playful squeeze.

"Let me show you the library. It's better than the one at Pembroke, if you can believe that. It's smaller, but...Well, you can tell me what you think." This was the place he'd longed to show her since he'd first seen her dorm room and realized what books meant to her. The library at Fox Hill would be a dream for a woman like Kat.

"It's really better than your dad's?"

"It is, but I plan to change the library when I'm in control of the estate. I want more first editions, more classics. We could have some stunning collector's items, and it could help draw visitors. There's a viscount my father knows who has an entire collection of Rudyard Kipling first editions. It draws a steady crowd to his estate every year. We could do the same at Pembroke."

"You really have it figured out, what you want to do when you become the earl?" Kat paused at the entrance to the library and watched him. Her gray eyes pierced clear through him, as though nothing could be hidden from her. Ancient eyes, yet so full of an intoxicating air of innocence. Tristan had never met anyone like her before in his life, and he'd opened up his heart to her, sharing his dreams with her.

I once had dreams, dreams my father crushed. But you've given me hope. He'd never imagined any woman would make him want to talk about his future and what he hoped he could do with his life, but Kat did.

The words could never be spoken. She'd never understand, and he couldn't show that vulnerability to her, not yet. Some things were too dark, too painful to share right away.

"Tristan?" Kat's voice called him back to the present.

"Sorry," he murmured, and joined her at the entrance to the library. "What did you say?"

"Your dad's estate, what's it like?"

He started to answer, but the distant sound of a doorbell chiming jogged his memory.

"Should we get that since Mr. Whitney isn't here?"

"Er...yes, I ought to." He covered her hand with his, and they walked away from the library back toward the front door.

"So, your father's estate, what's it like?" Kat pressed again.

Tristan rubbed his thumb over the back of her hand, reveling in how soft her skin was.

"Vast. There are miles of forest, fields, so much land. And the house is immense—tan stone, Georgian architecture. I wish—" He could never take Kat there. His father would ruin the last good thing he was trying to keep for himself.

"What?" Kat leaned in to him and gazed up with those lovely eyes, silently begging him to open up. The doorbell chimed again, and he scowled in irritation as they walked toward it.

"If my father weren't there, I'd take you."

Her brows furrowed. She seemed frustrated and hurt.

"It has nothing to do with you or what I think of you." He lifted her chin so he could see her eyes. "My father disapproves of *every* woman I've ever shown the slightest interest in, except Brianna Wolverton. He thinks he'll arrange my marriage to her and he'll get in the way of me and any woman I desire that he doesn't approve of." He sighed and pressed his forehead to hers again for a brief second before he backed away and opened the door, still looking at her as he spoke. "I don't ever want you to meet my father. He's cold, arrogant. Ruthless. He'll tear you down simply because I care about you. I want to protect you."

The frustration cleared from her expression, softening her gray eyes. "He's really that bad?"

"Worse. He'll do anything to make me come to heel. I don't want you anywhere near him."

"Well, you've already failed at that, boy." A cold voice sliced through Tristan.

He turned back to look at the open doorway, his hand still on the knob as he stared into the cold, arrogant face of his father, Edward Kingsley.

7

"**F**ather," he uttered harshly. His chest tightened and his hands clenched into fists as he struggled to remain calm.

He slowly moved to block Kat from his father's view. What the hell was his father doing at Fox Hill? He should have been back at the estate. Unless...he was furious that Tristan had returned to London and Kat, in which case...his father had tracked him down here.

Fucking hell.

Without so much as an "excuse me," his father pushed him out of the way and strode into the entrance hall, glowering.

"So, the rumors are true. Sleeping with the daughter of the man your mother married only this afternoon? Really, Tristan. I've taught you to control your urges better than that. Did you know they are calling you 'Lord of Scandal' back in London? Your picture and *hers*"—Edward nodded at Kat with a scowl—"are in every paper. Bloody TMZ was at the estate this afternoon hounding the guards at the front gates, asking about your affair with your stepsister." His father's voice grew louder as he talked, like a storm building upon the horizon.

Rather than shrinking behind Tristan as any other woman might when his father started to yell, Kat squared her shoulders and faced him, joining Tristan at his side.

"Father, get the bloody hell out of my house." His tone was ice-cold and he was one step away from shouting. It was one thing for Edward to attack him—he was used to being a target—but Kat was off-limits.

Edward chuckled. "Your house? Boy, this isn't—and never will be—*your house*. Just like everything else, what you think you own belongs to either your mother or me. The car you drive? Mine. The clothes on your back? Mine. The funds currently putting you through Cambridge? *Also mine*."

His father spat the last few words with such venom that it took every ounce of Tristan's control not to flinch.

"I own you, dear boy. Every part of you. Now, send that little American tramp back to London and come home with me to Pembroke immediately."

Kat's fingers curled around his, and he realized he'd balled them into fists and taken a step toward his father. Her touch gave him a strange mixture of strength and patience.

"I'm not sending her anywhere, Father."

A hard sneer covered his father's face. "Yes. You. Are. Because if you don't, you can say good-bye to everything I've given you. The car, the clothes, the program in Cambridge. Oh, and I'll sack Mr. Martin and his son, effective immediately."

"What?" Tristan hissed. Fury began to churn inside him, spinning madly.

This time his father smiled. "You wouldn't want to lose your beloved Carter and his father, would you? Without references from me, they'll be out of decent work. Lord knows what they'll have to do to make ends meet. After twenty-nine years of service, Mr. Martin will be cast out. No aristocratic family will dare to hire him, not when I've expressed my views on his poor job performance."

Tristan couldn't breathe. Carter and his father...tossed off the estate. Their entire lives were at Pembroke. He couldn't ruin that for...

Kat's hand fell away from his, and it felt like he was falling through a black tunnel, no end in sight. Just crushing darkness.

"You have one night, Tristan. Be back at Pembroke first thing tomorrow morning without her, or I'll destroy the Martins and take everything else you love away from you. Clear enough?" Edward straightened his suit, then pulled a pair of leather gloves out from his coat pocket and slid them on in a slow but controlled movement, like a military general.

Tristan's throat constricted, but he gave no sign to his father that he agreed. Everything inside him was raw and yet numb at the same time.

"Happy Christmas." His father's words were dark, and all too cold, given the season. An amusing parting shot, no doubt, as he ripped Tristan's world apart.

It was a long moment after his father left the house before Tristan recovered from the shock. Numbly, he walked slowly toward the library, the room in Fox Hill that he took the greatest comfort in. Kat followed silently, her eyes wide and face ashen. He leaned heavily against one of the reading tables, trying to clear his head of the thoughts rushing madly through his mind.

Kat had moved to stand in front of one of the large windows, hugging herself as she gazed out at the snow-covered gardens of Fox Hill.

"Kat..." Her name burned his lips.

She turned his way, and he glimpsed tears coursing down

her cheeks. She tried to smile, but it was more of a grimace. Was she dying inside like he was?

"I guess it's really over this time, isn't it?" She started to turn away again, but Tristan strode over and spun her, catching her against him.

If he held fast to her, he might not have to let her go. A foolish hope, but it was there all the same.

A muffled sob came from her, and she clung to him.

I have had everything a man could want my entire life. Until her. And she'll never belong to me...The one thing I—

He squeezed Kat tighter to him. Every moment of his life seemed to have led to this, and his father was taking her away.

"Tristan, I can't go back to my dad, not after what happened, but I can't stay here either."

The pain lancing through him flared his temper. "Why not? My father can't take you from me. He can't—"

Kat reached up to place a fingertip to his lips. "We both know he would do what he threatened to. And I'm not going to let you choose me, not when you know in your heart you have to protect Carter and his dad. It's the right thing to do."

"To hell with what's right. I want you, Kat. I don't need anyone but *you*."

When she pushed him away, it cut his soul in two.

"The man you are, the man I fell for, does the right thing, even when he doesn't want to. I know I teased you about being a bit high and mighty, but the truth is..." She rubbed her eyes, wiping away stray tears. "The truth is, you're one of the best people I've ever met. Even though you try to hide it, your heart is so full of love, for your mother, for Celia, Carter...The people you love are a part of what makes you so wonderful. I will not be the woman who steals them from your life."

Kat was killing him. His lungs tightened and his anger boiled to the surface.

"So you'll condemn me to the fate my father has planned? Don't tell me that you can sit back and watch me walk away. I'll have to marry someone else. That's what he wants. Political allies, a strategic marriage, a life of silent desperation. You would do that to me?"

How could she not see that if they gave in to his father's wishes this time, they'd lose each other and their chance at shared happiness? Edward Kingsley had played his trump card and wouldn't hesitate to exploit anyone to get anything he wanted.

"We have to grow up, Tristan. Not everything is a fairy tale. We had a glimpse of something few other people ever have in their entire lives. But we have to give it up because it's the right thing to do." Her voice was quiet but firm, and it cut his heart to ribbons.

There it was, that glimmer in her eyes of an ancient knowledge of having endured this before, in another life, another time. How could she be so brave? It was destroying him, but she stood tall in the face of losing their chance of being happy together. Everything they'd done today seemed a thousand years away, as though a stranger, not him, had experienced that joy, that freedom to just...*be* with the woman he cared about.

"We have one night. Let's not waste it." She held out a hand to him.

TRISTAN CURLED HIS FINGERS AROUND HERS AND TUGGED her toward him. Being in his arms was like coming home, the way she felt as a little girl, climbing down the steps of her bus and running across the thick summer grass, spying her house in the distance. The house she'd lived in as a child. Before her mother left...before everything changed.

She tilted her head back and gazed into Tristan's eyes.

One of us has to be strong enough to keep things together for one more day.

"Pretend with me," she breathed as she stood on tiptoe and brushed her lips against his.

"Pretend?" His hand gripped the back of her neck, lightly massaging away the knots of tension.

"Yes." Kat kissed him lightly. "Pretend it's just you and me. No one else exists in this world. What happens with this last day, it will *always* be ours. No one can take that away from us."

His mouth, usually so stern and proud, curved into a gentle, wry smile. Slowly, so slowly the anticipation drove her mad, Tristan lowered his head until their lips touched.

Sweet kisses, soft but firm hands stroking, a shared exhale...

It began to build, like the sky burning with shades of fire as the dawn approached. Kat gasped as Tristan suddenly lifted her up and she curled her legs around his waist. He carried her to a bookshelf that had a wide waist-high shelf. When she hit the wood, he pressed against her, his mouth devouring hers while his hands fumbled with the buttons of his jeans.

"Let...me..." She panted between searing kisses and hopped down to stand.

He stepped back and pulled his sweater off, tossing it away while she toed out of her boots and stripped out of her clothes. When she was down to her panties and bra, he was on her again, placing her back on the ledge. She wound her arms around his neck, stroking her fingers through his hair and tracing the shapes of his shoulder muscles. He was so beautiful.

My own fallen angel. She smiled against his lips.

Tristan kissed his way down to the tops of her breasts, and with a little tug on her bra, he freed them from the black cotton bra cups. One of his palms cupped her left breast, while his mouth closed over the peak of the right. Sucking hard on the tip, he tortured her sweetly. She writhed against the bookshelf behind her, feeling the spines of the old books rasping against her skin. Digging her hands into his hair, she tugged on the strands.

Rather than relent, he moved his lips down her belly. With a low growl, he ripped the panties off. The scraps dropped to the ground, and he flattened his palms on her inner thighs, shoving them wide apart. Kat let go of his hair so she could grasp the edges of the bookcase to keep herself from falling. He pressed kisses, feathery and light, followed by little love bites, against her inner thighs as he worked his way toward her mound. Kat shivered and arched against the shelf, gripping the wood to stay upright. She glanced down, seeing his dark hair glinting in the soft glow of the library light. Every kiss, every little stroking touch of his hands and lips upon her skin, set fire to her body.

Tristan's lips moved closer and closer to her mons, and her head spun a little when she realized where his mouth was headed. When he found her clit and he sucked on the sensitive bud, sparks shot through her, and she cried out at the harsh stab of arousal and the rush of wet heat. He licked her, kissed her, tortured her with his mouth until she was chanting—more like begging—his name in reverent breaths. The climax hit her slowly, softly, a cresting wave of pleasure, drawing her out to sea and lulling her into relaxing.

"Don't quit on me yet, darling." He chuckled as he rose and towered over her. He went to unbutton his jeans. Kat reached for him, but he caught her wrists and pinned them above her head with one of his hands. His other hand freed his cock and then positioned himself at her entrance. He kissed her hard, brutal almost, as he thrust into her body. She bit his lip as pleasure at the sudden invasion tore through her.

Nothing will ever feel this good again...

She could barely think coherently as he withdrew from her and then slammed back in. He kept her wrists pinned and her body open for his taking. Everything was too much, too overwhelming, the emotions, the sensations, the need to move and to feel him move inside her.

"Who do you belong to?" His voice was low, rough, and commanding.

Their gazes locked and the primal part of her British bad boy was there, like churning fires in the mouth of a volcano. And she wanted to be burned. Bad.

"You," she moaned. She arched her back, undulating her body against his. The savage sound that tore from his lips as he fully claimed her made her explode.

He pounded into her, relentless, their hips colliding with such force she knew she'd be bruised tomorrow. The bookcase rocked on its edges, the wood creaking in between the sounds of their bodies coming together. Several books crashed down to the floor around them, but neither of them cared.

"I'm yours, Tristan, forever," she whispered as he buried his face in her neck.

Then, as the orgasm fully knocked into her, she threw her head back. A second later Tristan cried out, his body rigid as he came. He let go of her wrists and clasped her face in his hands and kissed her, his breathing harsh. His chest pressed to hers and their hearts beat wildly. When their mouths broke apart, Kat had to catch her breath.

That was when she noticed that a portion of the upper library windows were stained glass. The middle panel depicted a medieval woman and man in an embrace. The vivid colors were glowing with the setting sun outside, and the couple seemed to come alive, love evident on their etched features. Beneath them was an inscription, and Kat murmured the words aloud.

"*Amor omnia vincit improbus.* What does it mean?" she asked him.

"What?" Tristan nuzzled her cheek, their bodies still joined.

"*Amor omnia vincit improbus,*" she repeated, her eyes drifting between his face and the medieval stained glass.

"Love conquers all."

When he spoke those words, she heard the pain buried just beneath the surface of his tone. She placed a hand on his cheek and stroked his jaw, the faint stubble scraping her skin.

Stay with me, Tristan. Don't lose control now.

They only had one night and they needed to fill it with a lifetime of memories.

8

Everything Kat had dreamed of but had been too afraid to hope for was ending tonight. As she held Tristan against her body, she clung to him like he was a fading phantom.

With a sigh, he pulled away from her. She watched him use a handkerchief to wipe himself and her before he fixed his trousers.

Kat slid off the shelf, her feet unsteady from the two overpowering orgasms. Using the bookcase as support, she grabbed her clothes, minus the ripped underwear, and dressed quickly.

Tristan didn't speak while she dressed, instead gazing at the stained-glass couple. When he finally faced her, his eyes were shadowed with sorrow.

"You asked me if the stained glass at my mother's town house was what moved me to tears. It wasn't." He lifted his head in the direction of the medieval couple. "It was them."

Love conquers all.

Kat blinked rapidly as unshed tears stung her eyes. "It's so beautiful."

He turned his gaze away from the medieval lovers and looked at her, those blue-green eyes casting a spell upon her heart.

"If we only have one night." The barest hint of a hitch in his voice stung her.

She struggled to breathe. "Then we should do something wonderful."

Tristan lifted his head, stark pain in his eyes. "You're mine and I'll do anything you want." The way he said *you're mine* sent little flutters through her chest.

Kat walked over to him and wrapped her arms around him. "I want to spend it with you. No one else. Let's not leave your bed until morning."

His responding smile warmed her insides.

Holding his hand, she followed him out of the library.

When they reached Tristan's room, she was surprised at the bittersweet melancholy that swept through her. She'd lost her virginity here, and she'd lost her heart to him that same night.

Warm hands settled on her waist as Tristan caught hold of her from behind and pulled her against him. He nuzzled her cheek and exhaled.

"We have so little time," he murmured.

Kat placed her hands on his and squeezed lightly. Her chest was tight as emotions flooded her.

"Tell me about Pembroke. The house I mean. You never really talk about it."

He stiffened behind her.

"Please, Tristan, forget your father. Just tell me about your home." She wanted—no, *needed*—to have a place to picture in her mind, so when she lay in bed at night, missing him, she could see him.

A small, almost hesitant smile touched his lips. "I have an

idea. Let's go out tonight for a little while. Let me show you what Christmas at Cambridge is like."

Christmas at Cambridge? With him? It would be perfect. She knew he was avoiding talking about his father's estate, most likely because he was upset by what Edward had done to them today. Yet Kat knew he needed to stop associating his father with the estate. Pembroke was to be his life, his future.

She turned in his arms and kissed him soundly. "I'd like that."

A boyish smile lit his face. "Dinner at a pub, King's College Choir, and maybe ice-skating?"

She laughed. "Sounds wonderful! Have you done all this before?"

His smile slipped. "After my parents separated, Mother and I started spending Christmas here. They are happy memories for me, coming here with her, just the two of us."

"I'm so sorry," she whispered. Her heart squeezed, and she trailed her fingertips over his sensual lips.

Tristan's smile was back. "Don't be. We'll make more memories tonight."

"New memories," she agreed. *Our last ones together.*

He led her downstairs to retrieve their coats, and they passed the butler, Whitney.

"We'll be out for the night, but will be back late. Don't wait up for us."

"Very good, sir," the butler said as they headed for the door.

They walked to Tristan's car, and he held the door open for Kat. They were quiet as he drove them into town. Dusk had settled around the sleepy snow-covered town, and most of the streets were empty. Glittering lights and holiday decorations were splashes of bright color against the white background. She'd been gone two weeks, and in that time Christmas had taken over.

"How about dinner at the Old Spring Pub? It's not fancy, but it's fun," Tristan suggested as he parked the car against the curb.

"Sounds great." Kat followed him to the little restaurant.

They found a table by the window. A slight chill from the cold glass made her shiver despite the fireplace nearby and the warmth of the pub's interior.

Tristan sat beside her rather than across from her, and he wrapped an arm around her shoulders. His body heat seeped into her, and she sighed.

This was heaven. A man she could call hers for one more night.

When a waiter came over, they ordered roast turkey and mince pie with brandy butter. "Oh, and chestnut soup to start," Tristan added.

"Why is it your food always sounds so good?" Kat nudged him playfully in the ribs.

He winked. "Better than pizza?"

"Better." She laughed and rested her head against his shoulder. "Now, would you please tell me about Pembroke? I know you were avoiding it before. But I need to hear about it. Please?" Sometimes opening up about things helped, and she thought asking him one more time was worth it. If he really didn't want to talk about his father's estate, then she'd let it go.

Tristan reached for one of her hands and linked his fingers through hers.

"I've lived most of my life at Pembroke. I know every nook, cranny, and dusty attic, but it doesn't feel like home. Father always reminds me it isn't mine, not until he dies. It's hard to love a place when someone stands in your way."

Kat squeezed his hand. "What if your father weren't part

of the equation? Take him out. Pretend it's just you running Pembroke. Is that something you could do for the rest of your life?" She wasn't trying to challenge him or his duty to his title; she was just curious. If Tristan were free to live his life, she wanted to know what he'd choose.

"I would choose Pembroke. Carter and I have been planning things for years. The estate is self-sufficient, but only just. It still needs a healthy source of income, and my father is too old-fashioned to embrace any ideas to bring Pembroke into the future."

She lifted her head and stared at him. True excitement gleamed in his blue-green eyes. He raised their joined hands and kissed her knuckles. The sweet gesture made her insides flutter in joy and pleasure.

"What would you do to modernize the estate?" she asked.

His eyes lit up. "That's the fun part. I'd open it up for film and TV crews. We'd get incredible exposure and be paid for location shooting. Then, of course, there would be tourists, busloads of them coming to see where everything was filmed. It could really define Pembroke's future. Open the gates, let the people come in and experience a true working British estate."

Kat instantly saw the appeal of his idea. He was right: Tourists would eat up the entire idea of visiting a filming location, as well as a home with a historical heritage.

"And your dad won't entertain the idea at all?" she asked carefully.

His lips wilted from a smile to a frown. "No. I've mentioned it, and he flatly refused to let tourists trample his beloved grounds. I didn't even have the chance to present my working plan on how Carter and I would implement changes and start making contacts with studios and tour companies." There was a frustration to his voice, and the shadows in his eyes told Kat how upset he was.

"It's not your fault that he won't listen to a brilliant idea when he hears one."

"Thank you, darling." He chuckled and pressed a kiss to her temple.

It stung her deep inside to think that a parent would discount a child's dream or ideas. Her father would never have done that. She'd talked his ear off about her plans to be a history professor. It wouldn't make a lot of money, but it was her calling. To give the students the gift of loving the past. For Tristan's father to callously put down his son's plan to secure the future of the family estate made her heart ache for him.

Their food arrived and they ate the delicious pub fare, talking about a thousand little things and laughing as outside a group of students ran past throwing snowballs at one another.

We won't talk about tomorrow. We can't.

"Finished?" Tristan squeezed her waist and eyed her mostly empty plate.

"Yeah, you?" She giggled at his immaculately clean plate.

"Mm-hmm. Let's see if we can catch King's College Choir." He left a couple of fifty-pound notes on the table, nodded at their waiter, and led her back out into the night. Their last night...

❦ 9 ❦

K at and Tristan navigated the narrow Elizabethan streets until they reached King's College. It was perhaps the most architecturally elaborate of all of the colleges at Cambridge, with its tall spires and large, sprawling edifices. They followed a crowd that was making its way through a set of doors leading into a chapel.

A choir of thirty white-robed boys and young men were flipping pages in their hymnals on wooden pedestals. Candles in clear glass hurricanes flickered, casting golden illumination upon the choir and the crowd.

Tristan led her to one of the end rows near the front, where they had a stunning view of the stained glass. The interior of the chapel, with its pillars stretching toward the heavens and feathering outward over the ceiling in exquisite slopes was breathtaking.

"Tristan, this is beautiful," she whispered.

He didn't respond except to kiss her lips and stroke a thumb over her mouth before he handed her a hymnal.

As the choir burst into song, the sounds echoed off the aged stone, and the effect was surreal. She curled her arm through his and rested her head against his shoulder. It felt like they were just another couple attending Christmas service. Cuddling, singing, celebrating the holidays. A normal guy and a normal girl.

She stifled a sigh. Tristan was anything but normal, but tonight she could pretend he was just her boyfriend, not the future Earl of Pembroke, and not her stepbrother.

Toward the end of the service, she noted that cameras on tripods were sweeping the crowd gathered for the service. One moved slowly past them, then drifted back and paused on them for nearly two minutes. The red light indicated it was recording, and Kat's heart jumped into her throat.

"Tristan," she whispered. "The cameras." She tilted her head at the one facing them.

"I know. They broadcast the service worldwide."

"Oh my God, what if someone sees us?" she gasped.

His boyish smile faded, and with a seriousness that shocked her, he replied, "Exactly." And then he grasped her waist and kissed her, right there in front of God and the world.

Long after she'd lost herself in his kiss, she came floating back to reality. The service was over, and people were shuffling past them, a few glaring at them, recognition flashing in their eyes. Tristan wouldn't let her go though, even when she felt embarrassment flood her face with heat.

"Let them look. I'm not ashamed to be with you, Kat. I never was." He brushed his fingertips over her jaw, down to her chin and up again to her lips.

He isn't ashamed of me. It felt so good to hear him say it. She hadn't wanted to let those self-deprecating thoughts inside her head, but they'd been there, buried by the sweet memories of his touch, his kiss. He wasn't trying to hide their relationship, or what few hours remained of it.

"Let's go skating. Then we have gifts to open." The boyish look was back.

This was what Tristan would've looked like if his childhood had been a happy one. The sardonic smiles and ruthless seductions would not have been second nature to him. Yet, tortured as he was with his painful family situation, he was perfect to her.

"What are you thinking about?" he asked as she swept her hair back from her shoulders.

Damn, the man was so sweet sometimes.

A lie was on the tip of her tongue, but she didn't want to lie to him.

"I was just thinking I'd give anything to have a normal life with you. No parents, no paparazzi, no peerage titles or fancy estates. Just us."

Shadowing his eyes was the grief of a man who'd learned long ago to give up what he wanted. Sacrificing his own happiness was in his blood, but he didn't want to do this any more than she did.

"That's a wish for another day. Another life." He stroked her lips again but didn't kiss her.

He was hurting deeply, like she was.

They exited the chapel and followed the shoveled sidewalks back out to the main streets. Neither of them spoke for several minutes. When they reached the ice rink, it was empty of the crowds she'd expected, but perhaps the families were at home, opening presents.

Tristan purchased two tickets, and they collected skates. Sitting down on a bench, Kat pulled her boots off and put on her blades. He was quicker, and knelt at her feet, jerking the white laces together, then tying them up.

She watched him, her heart so full her chest seemed fit to burst.

With a gentle tap of his fingers on her toes, he stood. "All set." Then he held out his hand to her as they walked toward the ice.

The second they were ready to step out, Kat clutched Tristan's arm.

"I may have forgotten to mention that I don't know how to ice-skate."

Tristan chuckled. "I get the pleasure of taking your skating virginity as well? Excellent!" He clapped his hands together like an overeager schoolboy, and the look of sheer delight on his face was enchanting, and sexy as hell.

She couldn't resist smacking his chest.

"You're a bastard," she whispered, but tugged him down to kiss him soundly.

"Come on, Scaredy-Kat," he teased, and stepped onto the ice, pulling her with him.

Every bone in Kat's body was rigid as she followed him. The ice gleamed, its slickness looking treacherous, but Tristan curled an arm around her waist.

"Feet apart," he instructed, using his body as a guide. "Straighten your back a little, but lean forward slightly. It's all about balance and strong ankles." He bent his legs in at the knees, but kept his ankles straight.

She imitated the stance. He was right. Kat felt a lot steadier like that.

Tristan held out a hand and she took it. "Keep that position and I'll pull you."

"Okay." She held her free hand out, keeping her body balanced, and Tristan started to skate. His powerful legs kicked across the ice, the soft *scrape-scrape* noise echoing against the white waist-high walls of the rink.

He pulled her along by the hand for a few minutes before he suddenly let go. She sucked in a breath as she coasted past him and wobbled to a stop on her own. Kat turned around, arms flailing a little, and scowled at him.

Tristan was watching her, arms crossed, a wicked smile on his lips.

"How about a game?" he asked.

"Oh, no! Whatever you're thinking, stop!" But she started to laugh as he prowled across the ice, digging the pointed end of his skates in like a mountain climber's boots.

"If you can catch me, I'll let you be in charge in bed tonight. If you can't catch me, I'm the master tonight." The grin he flashed was dangerous, and it made her shiver with desire.

"Master?"

"Yes, as in I tell you what to do, and you do it. Or else I might have to punish you."

Kat had heard of role-playing games. She may have been a virgin, but it wasn't as though she hadn't read romance novels before. The idea of playing something like that with him? Tristan as the master? Her body flamed at the thought. Not a bad way to spend the night. She stifled a giggle.

"I have to catch you?" she clarified.

"Right. And if you don't try hard enough, I'll make it devilishly hard for you, darling. I might have to bring you to the edge over and over before I let you come. So don't think to play it easy. Come after me." That smile got bigger as he watched her process what he'd said.

The idea had her entire body flushing with so much heat, she actually felt beads of sweat dewing on her skin.

"Oh yeah?" she called out breathlessly.

"Yes. I might order you to lie flat on your back and hold very, *very* still while I go down on you. Maybe I'll have to bind your hands so you can only enjoy what I want to do to you."

Those silken suggestions were irresistible.

Her thighs clenched and her abdomen quivered with desire at the thought of his mouth on her down there, his tongue flicking against her and...

"I'll give you a full minute to catch me. Sporting chance and all that." He winked and skated backward.

Kat braced herself and used her legs to propel herself forward. He dared to skate close a few times, teasing her, taunting her with wicked whispers of how much he wanted her on her knees, her lips wrapped around his cock, sucking him off, how he wanted to make her ride him cowgirl style. A thousand things that made her blush and had her body heating with excitement.

After a few close calls where his clothing was just within a few inches of her grasping hands, she realized she needed to outsmart Tristan. When she wobbled and almost face-planted, a brilliant idea struck.

She waited until he swished past her and lunged as if trying to catch him, before letting gravity do what it did best. With a squeak of mock surprise, Kat fell on the ice. Pain aside, it was a genius plan. She didn't have to fake the agony as she clutched one of her ankles.

"Kat!" Tristan was bearing down on her, sliding into a fancy hockey stop inches from her.

She held her breath, and the second he crouched beside her, she launched herself at him, tackling him onto his back.

"Gotcha!" she panted, laughing at the shocked look on his face.

Blue-green eyes wide, brows arched up, he just blinked at her. "You sneaky little colonist!" He broke into a grin as he gripped her waist, keeping his hold on her body, letting her lie atop him.

"Hmm...Should I dump some tea into your harbor?" She flashed him a coquettish look, batting her lashes and licking her lips.

Tristan burst out laughing. "What does that even mean?"

Heat flooded her cheeks and she ducked her head. "I have no idea. I thought it sounded dirty."

He cupped her face and gave her a nipping kiss. "Bloody hell, woman, I adore you." Tristan chuckled, the words soft, a little rough, as he continued to laugh.

Her heart turned over in her chest, and she couldn't resist kissing him back.

It was a playful kiss, full of light and heat, like warming one's hands in front of a fire in winter. She wanted to tell him so much, everything she felt deep inside, but those words would bring tears. She refused to cry tonight.

"Oi! No snogging, you two!" A gruff man in a thick winter coat leaned over the rink railing, frowning.

Kat rolled off Tristan, her face flaming, but she couldn't keep a smile off her face.

Tristan leaned in close to her when she sat up on the ice. "He's right. Snogging is much better at home." He winked. "I'll want you naked when I obey all your commands."

"You're terrible, you know that?" She shoved at his shoulder.

"Terribly charming? Terribly sexy?"

She snorted. "You know exactly what you are."

"And you like that about me." He kissed her cheek and helped her to her feet.

As they skated back to the edge of the rink, Kat caught a glimpse of a man with a camera, his lens aimed in their direction.

"Tristan, I think that guy took photos of us." She pointed, an anxious knot suddenly forming in her stomach.

"Probably followed us from King's College," Tristan muttered. "Oh well. What harm could it do? The news is already all over London, and your father knows about us as well." They stopped at the benches and hastily removed their skates and put their shoes back on before leaving the rink.

Kat hated to think that her relationship with Tristan was

so public. She'd never been infamous for anything before, and it made her feel jittery.

Tristan pulled her to a stop on the sidewalk and cupped her cheek.

"Don't let it bother you. I know that seems impossible, but they'll lose interest as soon as the next scandal happens."

The idea of her personal life on display made her stomach turn, but she wasn't sure it could be prevented. Tristan had to deal with this every day. His playboy past and the attention the press put on him wasn't something he'd sought out. The paparazzi forced it upon him.

She and Tristan left the ice rink and drove back to Fox Hill. Whitney was there to meet them, smiling a little as he took their coats.

"The frosting has dried which means the cookies are ready for you and the young lady."

"Thank you, Whitney. Happy Christmas." Tristan shook the butler's hand before he led Kat to the kitchen.

"Why don't you get dessert and I'll fetch the presents," he said. "Do you remember the room opposite the billiard room? That's the TV room. I'll meet you there."

"Okay. My present for you is in my duffle," Kat called as he started to vanish through the doorway, her smile fading a little as he turned away. After he was gone, she leaned back against the counter and struggled to deal with the rising sorrow.

We have only a few more precious hours. And I'm going to make it count.

🪳 10 🪳

Tristan held two small wrapped parcels as he strode down the hall toward the TV room

He found her nestled on the couch with two small plates of cookies in her hands. A fire roared in the redbrick fireplace. The scene was welcoming, homey, and with Kat sitting there waiting for him, he was having trouble walking due to his sudden state of arousal.

"You look good enough to eat," he murmured as he joined her on the couch.

The soft, breathless laugh she gave warmed him inside. "Charmer." She handed him his plate, then kissed him.

"I'm *your* charmer." He brushed the back of his knuckles over her cheek.

They ate their cookies in a pleasant silence that fascinated him. *She* fascinated him. It wasn't just the sex, although he'd told himself that at first. It was everything about her. Just sitting next to her on the couch and eating decadent chocolate, listening to the snap and crack of the logs in the hearth, was magical.

"Let me take the dishes." He rose from the couch and

carried the plates to a nearby table. When he returned to the couch, he cuddled her against him and placed his present in her lap.

"Go on, open it." Tristan curled his arm around her shoulders as he watched her carefully unwrap the gift to reveal a small black velvet box. Her eyes lifted to his, questioning.

"I know you don't normally wear something like this, but I thought it might be worthy of an exception."

She bowed her head as she cracked open the box and her little gasp made his heart race. It had taken him a week to acquire this present. He'd hoped to win her back, to show her how much he believed in her, how much he adored her. It was supposed to be a promise of what their future could be. Butterflies and stained glass. Seemingly fragile, but outlasting everything.

"Tristan..." She whispered his name, emotion breaking her voice slightly. Kat lifted her gift out of the box and held it up. It was a gold bracelet with seven charms hanging from the links. Each one was a tiny butterfly, their wings shimmering with the color of precious gemstones. The eighth charm was a small pendant carved with the Pembroke family crest.

"I wanted to give you butterflies that would never die." *And a piece of me to take with you.*

When she turned to look at him, the bracelet clenched in her fist, he came undone at the expression in her eyes. There it was again. That look of a princess born in a garden who lived her life among the colorful blooms. Yet there was a sadness in her expression that tore at his heart. Their dreams would not come true.

My dream. The haze of a growing pain spread in his chest. *I won't ever be able to have her in my life, not in the way I wish.*

"How are you so perfect?" she whispered, her words catching. "Why couldn't you be someone I could live without?"

Did she know she'd said that aloud?

"I can only be me, Kat. And right now I'm the man who *loves* you." His admission startled him, but his words were true, pure, no hesitation.

I love her. I've loved her for as long as I've known her. How is that even possible?

"You love me?" Tears clung to her lashes.

He nodded, his throat tight as he swallowed a flood of emotions.

"Oh, Tristan, this is awful!" she cried out, and buried her face in his chest, her arms curled around his neck as she wept. The sound of Kat's sobs tore him apart.

"Awful?" Too stunned to do anything else, he simply held her as she sobbed.

"Yes," she whispered. "I love you, too. Why can't the world just let us be?"

"Because life is a cruel mistress." He knew that better than most, wishing with every breath in his body he could take her pain into himself and endure it for her.

When Kat dried her eyes and looked at him again, a false smile stretched her lips.

"You need to open your present." She handed him her own wrapped package. "I thought about buying you a map, but when I saw this...I thought it would be better than a hundred maps."

His hands shook as he ripped the red shiny paper away to reveal an antique rosewood box. When he opened the lid, his heart skipped a beat. A brass nautical compass sat inside. The arrow continued to point north as he rotated the box slightly.

"I want you to always find your way in life, Tristan. Your dad isn't going to make things any easier on you, and I wanted you to remember that only you can live your life. Maybe it will keep you heading to your true north." She cupped his cheeks. Her hands were so warm, and they trembled against his face.

"I won't ever stop loving you, Kat. Tell me you believe me." He needed to hear her say it. All this time, his reputation had kept her on edge, and it'd cost them so much. All he wanted now was for her to hear the truth and believe him.

She nodded, eyes glimmering. "I believe you. I love you, too. I've never been in love before, but I know that's what this pain is inside me." She laughed a little, but the sound was hollow. "From the moment I saw you that night in the pub, I've been under a strange and wondrous spell. A love spell. No matter what happens tomorrow or years from now, my heart is yours." Kat placed his hand against her chest above her heart and swallowed thickly.

So this is what it feels like to love something and lose it forever?

"Make love to me, Tristan. Make me forget everything but us." She lifted his hand and kissed his palm.

That silent desperation lurked under his skin again, rippling through him as he sought to quell the rising anger and panic at the thought of losing Kat. He rose from the couch and shut the door to the TV room, sealing them in. Then he pointed to the thick white rug by the fire. Kat left the couch and stood on the carpet.

There was so much about tonight he wanted to savor, to permanently press into his memory so he could never forget it.

She slipped out of her boots and socks, and when she started to lift her sweater up, Tristan caught her hands and took over the task himself, pulling it off her. Kat shivered as the cool air hit her bare skin and her nipples puckered against the white cotton bra she wore. How something so sweet and modest could affect him so strongly was a mystery.

She seemed to realize he wanted to undress her and made no move to do the rest on her own. Tristan knelt on one knee as he pulled her jeans down and she stepped out of them. His face was level with her navel, and he couldn't resist kissing the slight curve of her belly.

Her hands fluttered before settling in his hair as he kissed her skin. She was warm and soft, and that sweet feminine scent that was all Kat sent an aching hunger through his very bones.

All we have is tonight.

It will never be enough.

Slowly, he hooked his fingers in the lace edge of her panties and tugged them down, baring her sex. He smoothed his hands up her calves, her thighs, and then he grasped her full bare bottom, squeezing gently.

"Tristan, I want *you* naked." Her words were breathless, and excitement glittered in her eyes. She was an open book, his to read, to memorize, to *live* with, at least for one more night.

He stood and reached around behind her to unfasten her bra. She caught the cups before they fell and raised one delicate brow in challenge.

"Your turn, Kingsley." She'd never called him that before, but he liked it.

"As you wish," he replied smoothly, and her lashes fluttered. He knew she loved his voice. He wasn't about to forget something that turned her on.

Kat reached for a few pillows from the couch and sat down by the fire while he stripped out of his clothes. The moment he was naked, he came toward her, slow, deliberate, letting no part of tonight escape his memory. Her hair curled slightly at the ends and kissed the tops of her breasts as she tossed the bra away and scooted back on the carpet to lie against the pillows. He crawled up her body, kissing and nuzzling every inch of her skin. He took his time, savoring her taste and the way little strokes of his fingers along her sensitive skin made her shiver and her breath quicken. He wanted to be inside her, but he didn't want to rush this either. Kat met his gaze, her eyes full of understanding. She needed this slow, too. There was still so much he wanted to tell her, to ask her, to know before they had to...He banished the thought before the stinging pain could set in and lowered his lips to hers.

The kiss was tender at first, delicate and sweet, but then it deepened as the fire between them ignited. He cupped her face with one hand, brushing his thumb over her cheekbone as he possessed her lips, drinking in her sweet taste. A heady sense of wild joy mixed with a hungry desperation overrode his control. This wasn't just sex. He'd been a fool to ever think what lay between him and Kat could be so simple. No, this was a thing of infinite wonder, the greatest gift he could ever have. A woman who loved him, even the shadows in his heart.

"Tristan, you don't need to be gentle with me. I want you. Be my bad-boy Brit." Kat teased him with a little smile.

Despite the ache in his chest, his cock hardened further and his arousal spiked. "You want bad? That I can do, darling. Wait here." He leaped up, completely naked, and ducked out of the TV room wearing nothing but a blanket around his hips. Whitney had better not see him like this; he didn't want to have to explain.

He got to his room and dug around the top drawer of his nightstand, grabbing a few items he knew Kat had never experienced. Chuckling, he hastened back down the stairs and to the TV room. She was still lying there on the carpet, body gloriously bare for his gaze. The peaks of her breasts, the full hips, and curvy muscled legs. A goddess.

He held up the items he'd brought: a bullet vibrator and a pair of leather handcuffs lined with fur.

Her eyes widened and she stared at the cuffs and licked her lips. "You weren't kidding about the toys."

Tristan walked over to her, dropped the blanket, and knelt in front of her. "I never kid about sex toys, darling. Wrists," he demanded with a low growl.

When she hesitated the barest second, he arched a brow. "You cheated when you caught me skating tonight. I believe that entitles me to play the master tonight. Wrists," he repeated. His heart was pounding with excitement as she surrendered her hands and he placed the cuffs around her wrists.

"Good. Now lie back and reach over your head to grab the leg of the couch. You're not to let go, no matter what I do," he ordered.

"Mmm-kay," she murmured, her face a little red, and he could see by the way she was breathing faster that she was nervous.

"You trust me?" Tristan cupped her chin and forced her to meet his gaze.

"Yes." There was no hesitation as she did as he asked.

The position of her body left her bare to him and anything he wanted to do to her. Pressing his palms on the insides of her knees, he urged her to open her thighs. When she did, he turned on the small bullet vibrator and slipped it inside her.

"Oh!" Kat gasped and wriggled.

Tristan pressed her legs open wider and settled his upper body between her legs so he could press kisses to her mound and work his way down to her clit. The light whir of the vibrator hummed as he got closer, and Kat's legs trembled against his biceps. Her cuffed hands started to lift away from the couch.

He smacked the side of her arse lightly. "Put them back," he growled.

With a frustrated whimper, she dropped her hands back to the ground above her head, curling her fingers in a white-knuckled grip against the furniture leg.

To reward her, he fastened his lips around her clit and sucked on the sensitive bud. She cried out, wriggling at the overwhelming need to get away and get closer at the same time. The stimulation was too much, and he knew this was the first time she'd ever played a game like this.

"Come for me, beautiful." His command was followed by Kat's entire body jerking beneath him as an orgasm swept through her. It was a thing of beauty, to watch her come apart, the way a dozen emotions from surprise, to joy, then to delighted exhaustion passed over her features as she went limp. From her little nose, which was slightly upturned at the end, down to her pale-pink lips curving in a dazed smile, it all fascinated him.

I'll never get enough of her.

He carefully removed the bullet and turned it off. Then he removed the leather cuffs and massaged her wrists.

"Ready for me?" he asked in his voice gruff. If he couldn't get inside her soon, he was going to go mad. His cock was painfully hard, and every muscle in his body was aching for release.

"Yeah." Her breathless reply was all he needed.

Tristan rolled her onto her back, and she parted her legs further. When he slid inside her, that dark heat surrounded him, making him feel a thousand explosions of pleasure both physical and emotional. Their breaths mingled as they moved together, slow at first, the rhythm tender. But desperation and raw passion overtook them, sweeping them away.

He clasped her hands in his and pinned them on either side of her head as he thrust inside her. Kat lifted her chin, and he saw glints of light spark in her eyes as she started to come undone.

The sight brought him to the edge, but it wasn't until she whispered, "I love you," that he launched over into the rush of pure ecstasy.

Her name escaped his lips in a soft cry, and he buried his face in her neck afterward.

Bodies trembling, they clung to each other.

"What's your favorite childhood memory?" she asked, her voice gentle.

He stroked a hand along her outer leg, tracing patterns on her flesh, making her shiver.

"My favorite memory?" He considered the question. A spark of recollection, one sharp and almost painful, dug into the deepest part of his heart.

"Yes." Kat threaded her fingers through his hair, soothing him in ways she'd never know.

It took him a moment to catch his breath, to find the words.

"My father took me to Kensington Gardens when I was five. Just the two of us. That was years before the divorce..." That day flooded back, his father chasing him around the base of the Peter Pan statue. There had been a single moment when the sun had caught the edge of Peter's flute and Tristan had cried out.

"Papa, a fairy, look!"

And his father had caught him in his arms, laughed, and ruffled a hand through Tristan's hair. "So London still has some magic, eh?"

That was the memory he held on to, the man who dared to believe life still held some magic and mystery, that not all of life was full of disappointments. But something had changed in his father when Tristan had turned thirteen. Carter's mother had died, and the house was so heavy with grief that even Edward was affected. His parents divorced not long after, and his father had lost that last bit of humanity that had made him likable. Tristan hadn't given this change much thought, but now it stirred at the back of his mind, worrying him a little. What had changed his father into the hard-hearted man?

Tristan sighed. "He was a better man back then, not so cold. Distant, yes, but not cruel," he told Kat as he settled a hand on her hip and met her gaze. "What about you?"

She bit her lip, making him want to kiss her, but he needed his answer.

"It's when I was ten, two years before Mom left. She was out running errands, and I snuck up to the attic and found her old wedding dress." An unguarded smile curved her lips. "I don't know how I got it on, but I did. She came home and found me wearing it. I thought she'd be mad, but instead she spent the next hour playing dress-up with me. We got out all her jewelry and we did our hair. It was a mess, but it was fun. We laughed so hard it made my stomach hurt."

Seeing the flash of bittersweet pain in her eyes called out to every instinct inside him to protect her. Losing her mother had hurt Kat so much. He still had his father in his life, but she'd been abandoned.

Tristan lay beside her and pulled her flush to him. "Promise me you'll always remember you deserve to be loved." He twined a lock of her hair around his finger, focusing on her lips, then her eyes. "We are not our parents. We don't carry those sins and burdens. We can choose to love. No matter what happens tomorrow, don't ever forget that."

She nodded and pulled her head down to his.

There beside the warm fire, Tristan fully surrendered his heart to the only woman he would ever love. It would all shatter come the dawn.

But wasn't that how love was supposed to be? A wondrous risk that not all hearts survived? And Kat was worth it.

❧ 11 ☙

Kat couldn't breathe. The moment had come to say good-bye.

She and Tristan sat inside his car, parked in front of Lizzy's town house. The air between them was charged with tension thick enough to fog the windows.

They'd barely spoken since they'd left Cambridge earlier that morning. Part of her desperately wanted to believe this was all a dream and that they were still in bed, bodies entwined as they shared dreams.

The time for dreams was over.

"Tristan," she whispered, his name scraping across her vocal chords.

He furrowed his brow and clenched his jaw, his hands white-knuckled on the steering wheel.

"I'll walk you to the door." Tristan finally unbuckled his seat belt and got out of the car.

She followed him as he carried her duffle bag up to the front door of the town house. He set the bag down and shoved his hands into the pockets of his knee-length black coat.

I hate good-byes.

Tears were already forming in her eyes, burning and cutting like daggers straight to her heart. Kat was taking every memory of him with her, burying it safe within her. Someday soon they would cross paths again, but they both knew this thing between them could never be. Doomed from the start. She would always love him. Something this deep, this powerful, could never be undone.

Tristan pulled his hands from his pockets and reached for her cheek hesitantly, as though afraid to touch her. When he finally did, she tilted her head into his palm, closing her eyes for a few seconds.

"I won't say good-bye. I know you don't like them. But know that wherever I am, whatever I'm doing, I'll love you with every breath, every heartbeat. Always. You can't say good-bye to the one who owns your heart." He smiled, but it made her eyes flood with tears.

"No good-byes," she vowed. *God, I'm not going to survive this.* She couldn't breathe. Her lungs squeezed every breath out of her.

"Every night I'm going to close my eyes and remember our last night at Fox Hill." His eyes were dark and deep, like a northern sea in the coldest winter. Emotions churned in their depths and he blinked, swallowed hard, and continued, his voice rough, almost broken. "I'll tell myself I'll see you in the morning, because if I don't..." Tristan's throat worked as he struggled to swallow again.

Agonizing pain exploded through her, yet she didn't move, *couldn't* move. She understood what he was saying. He'd use that thought, that sweet little lie, to keep himself going. It was better than a good-bye, but only just.

Her heart jumped into her throat as she tried to tell him everything in her heart.

"I'll never love anyone the way I love you. You're my

first...my last." *And I have to be strong, because if I'm not, neither of us will get through this.* Kat stood on tiptoe and kissed him, curling her arms around his neck one last time.

Their mouths brushed gently before the fire lit between them and he was dragging her closer, crushing her to him. A sob choked her, but she didn't want to let go.

When they finally broke apart, Tristan's eyes were bright with tears.

"I can't bloody do this!" He shoved himself back a step with a curse, scraped his hand over his jaw, and then turned away, rushing down the steps to his car.

Tristan paused at the driver's side door, one hand braced on the roof of the Aston Martin as he looked over his shoulder at her. His beautiful face, those sharp, godlike features usually too perfect, were ravaged with the devastation of his breaking heart.

Something strange, almost eerie filled Kat as she gazed back him. It was as though someone had stepped over her grave...and her first thought was that she might never see him again.

"Tristan!" she cried out, but he was already climbing into the car and speeding away.

Kat didn't know how long she stood at the top of Lizzy's town house steps, the cold eating away at her bones. That terrible feeling of uneasiness wouldn't go away, like dark storm clouds were gathering thick upon the horizon.

I can survive this. I have to. She just had to convince herself of that.

She lifted the duffle bag up over her shoulder and pressed the little bell by the door. It was still early in the day, and she hoped her dad and Lizzy wouldn't be upset that she was just showing up without calling.

The door flew open and her father, not the butler, stood

there. Lines of worry and fear cut across his face, making him look years older than he should.

"Thank God!" he breathed, and opened his arms to her. That simple fatherly gesture of comfort and protection was the last thing she could handle.

The dam holding all of her pain and the raging emotions burst wide open.

"Dad!" The word came out of her in a hoarse cry. Kat dropped her bag and fell into his arms.

"Clayton? What's happened?" Lizzy's voice barely cut through the sound of Kat's sobbing as she burrowed into her dad's arms.

"I don't know, Lizzy. She's back. My baby's home."

She felt her father's lips brush her forehead, and she sagged against him in exhaustion, gasping softly for air.

"Why didn't you return any of my calls? We were worried sick. Neither you nor Tristan were picking up." Her father's question made her cringe with a new wave of pain. She had ignored his calls, and she knew Tristan had, too. They hadn't wanted their parents to destroy the last day they'd had together.

"I'm sorry we didn't answer you. We went to Cambridge." She closed her eyes briefly, drawing in a deep breath.

"Where's Tristan?" Lizzy asked

Kat lifted her head and finally looked her way. "Gone...His dad found us at Fox Hill. He threatened to..." She swallowed thickly. "To fire Carter and his dad and destroy their lives unless Tristan came home and never saw me again." Lizzy had told her this would happen, but Kat had never believed Edward would actually do something so horrible.

Lizzy's head dropped and her eyes darkened to a defeated shade of blue.

"I'm so sorry, Kat." Tristan's mother joined her and Clayton, embracing them both. "You have us, sweetheart," she promised. "We're both here for you."

Kat's heart shattered. She shut her eyes, fighting off fresh waves of pain. The emotions breaking apart inside her reminded her of when she'd accidentally knocked a glass vase off a table. The vase had splintered and fractured into hundreds of pieces on the floor, glittering in the late-afternoon light. Like the vase, Kat's dreams were shattered, too...

I'll never love anyone the way I love you.

She shut her eyes and saw Tristan at Fox Hill.

There is only love between us, no matter the time or distance. There is only love.

☙❦❧

"You're really not going back to class?" Carter leaned forward in his chair in Tristan's study at the Pembroke estate. "The new term starts in a few days."

Tristan shuffled the stack of reports on the estate's financial standings before he looked at his friend. Had it really been two weeks since Christmas? Tristan had buried himself in work after he and Kat had said their good-byes, and he'd lost track of time.

"No. I need to be here." His tone came out wooden because everything inside him was hollow. He'd been like this for days. A walking shell speaking only when necessary. It wasn't like before, when losing Kat had left him miserable. He'd felt sure then that he'd find a way to win her back.

That wasn't possible now. He'd won her and had been robbed of her. There was no going back. Life was over. It was that simple. His father had ripped apart his soul and left him to slowly die from the pain.

"Tristan, what's the matter? Talk to me." Carter's earnest

voice didn't move him. Nothing could. He stood and started to walk around his desk.

"I don't need a degree. It was a foolish idea. Now, if you'll excuse me, I need to—"

Slam!

Tristan hissed in pain as Carter shoved him against the wall and got in his face.

"Bloody hell, man. What's the matter with you? Ever since you came back you've been like..." Carter paused, his dark brown eyes almost as black as onyx stones.

"Been like what?" Tristan demanded coldly.

"Like your father."

Through the hollowness, anger exploded. Tristan shoved Carter back and swung a fist. The punch took them both by surprise.

Carter clutched his jaw, breathing hard as he fell back to lean against the desk. Tristan shook out his hand, ignoring the pain in his knuckles. He glanced away, unable to meet his friend's eyes for a moment. The anger had been replaced by a sweeping tide of guilt.

"Carter," he rasped, unsure of what to say. He'd *never* hit his friend before. He'd never wanted to either.

Carter winced as he let go of his jaw, but he smiled. "It's about time the real you came out swinging. Whatever happened over Christmas, you've got to fight back. No more rolling over."

Tristan shook his head. "It's not that simple. I lost her. Forever. My father found the one thing he can use to keep me away from her."

"What?"

"I can't talk about it. What Kat and I had can never be. And I'll never be able to tell her how much I..." The words choked him, and he couldn't go on.

"She knows you love her." Carter straightened his sweater,

smoothing it out.

Tristan leaned back against the wall, new pain filling his chest.

"She does, but it isn't enough. What I feel goes beyond words. I want to be with her, prove to her I love her. But my father won't let me near her." He didn't dare mention the real reason he and Kat had split up. To keep Carter's and his father's jobs safe. "I just want to tell her how much I care about her one more time, a grand public gesture or something." He laughed bitterly. "Sounds bloody over-romantic I know, but not being with her is driving me mad."

Carter stroked his jaw gently. "Everyone in London is talking about you two. Why not use the papers to your advantage for once?"

"How do you mean?"

With a shrug and a smile, his friend continued. "Your father hates negative press. Why not turn the tables on him? Bring a reporter inside Pembroke, tell them about you and Kat, how you fell for her. Show that soft side, and they'll eat it up. Your father won't be able to squash a love story. Hell, it might make him look better, too. You'll have the chance to make that grand public gesture for her. It might even make your father reconsider keeping you apart. If all of England is rooting for your relationship with Kat, it will be difficult for him to fight an entire country. You saw how everyone rooted for Kate Middleton when she and William dated. Brilliant, that was. Of course, she wasn't an American...but well..." Carter grinned. "You do like a challenge don't you?"

The idea was a good one, but then again, Carter was always the man with a plan. The positive press of a love story with a happy ending would be far better for his father's political agenda than another story of Tristan clubbing and charming his way into the beds of more women he'd never marry. This could actually work. For the first time in days, hope surged through him, filling him with new energy.

"I trust you know who to call to arrange an interview?" Carter asked.

Nodding, Tristan strode over to his desk, sifting through the stacks of papers until he found the business card with Jillian Jacobs's contact info.

Carter paused in the study doorway, tapping the door-frame with a hand as he glanced back at Tristan.

"Good luck. I'll be at Fox Hill if you need me."

And just like that, Carter left him alone. Tristan wanted to follow him. A thousand things had been left unsaid between them, but he needed to act fast. Kat would be headed back to Cambridge in a few days for the start of the new term, and he wanted her to see what he was about to do. A love letter, as best as he could manage, in front of the world, one he hoped would win over the country and convince his father to change his mind. He retrieved his phone and dialed.

"Jillian Jacobs," the photographer said.

"Ms. Jacobs, it's Tristan Kingsley."

"Mr. Kingsley! I'm so glad you called. I've been a bit afraid to speak to you after the photos went public. I honestly didn't know the campaign would be so big, and I didn't believe I'd win."

He exhaled and rubbed his temples. "I would have appreciated a warning. Kat and I are in a bloody tight spot over this mess."

"I'm so sorry—"

"You can make it up to me, Ms. Jacobs. I'd like for you to come to Pembroke today. Bring your camera."

"What?" Jillian stuttered.

Tristan leaned back in his chair, finally feeling more in control of his life than he had in a long time. "I plan to do an exclusive interview, and I wish for you to take the photos. Do you know any writers for *Monarch Magazine*? I believe they would be very interested in what I have to say about my relationship with Kat Roberts."

The photographer hesitated, but when she replied, her voice was breathless with excitement. "An exclusive with Tristan Kingsley? Given the current press about you and your stepsister? Yes, I'll have no trouble finding someone."

"Excellent. I'll expect you in two hours. I'll let my father's security at the gate know you're coming."

After he disconnected the call, he eased back into his desk chair and reached for the brass compass Kat had given him for Christmas. He opened the rosewood box and gazed down into the interior, watching the needle waver slightly but continue pointing north. Pointing toward Kat, toward his destiny.

It was two weeks into the new semester, and Kat still felt numb inside, the same way she'd felt when Tristan had left her on Lizzy's doorstep Christmas morning.

Numb and unable to breathe.

Unmoved, unfeeling, and with a drag to her steps, she barely got to her classes before the professors started their lectures. She was like a zombie. Kat walked straight from the dorm to her classrooms and back again. She only bothered to eat when the aching dull pit that formed in her stomach was too harsh to ignore. All around her the world seemed...faded. As though every bit of color and life had been drained from it. Nothing caught her eye; nothing made her heart race anymore.

She shivered as she stared out the classroom window, watching some of the other students throw snowballs at one another. They were running across the white-covered lawns, which was technically forbidden, but the wintry weather had made the professors less strict about the rules.

Flashes of her chasing Tristan across the ice rink slashed

through her. Such joy, such agony...It cut deep enough that she gasped aloud.

"Are you okay?" Lacy, her best friend, murmured from beside her in class. Worry lines creased around her eyes.

Kat jerked her gaze away from the window and realized several of the other students were watching her as well, eyes alight with curiosity.

"I'm fine," she lied, and dropped her eyes to the pages of her textbook, not reading a single word.

The professor was at the whiteboard writing the chapters for their next assignment, but Kat just let the words on the board blur as that deadness set in again.

The rumors about her and Tristan had eventually reached Cambridge, and she'd had to get used to the flashing cameras, shouted questions, and the mobs following her about the city. She no longer felt the sting of her classmates staring at her. Their interest in her personal life wasn't negative. Rather, everyone had seemed fascinated that she and Tristan had been dating and kept it a secret for as long as they had.

Headlines from newsstands jumped out at her with things like KINGSLEY'S BREAKUP WITH STEPSISTER SADDENS LONDON and WILL LONDON'S GREATEST CHARMER GET HIS AMERICAN SWEETHEART BACK? Every time she saw them, something inside her twisted in fresh pain before she sank back into the murky depths of her new unfeeling world. No one knew why they'd split up, and that had been the hardest part. Dodging the truth of the situation. For Carter's and his father's sake.

The professor dismissed the class, and Kat slung her backpack onto her shoulders, automatically heading for the door.

"It's going to be okay, Kat," Lacy said, walking next to her as they exited the building.

"Thanks," Kat replied halfheartedly. That was the trick

she'd learned. If she didn't feel, then she couldn't feel Tristan's loss. It didn't always work.

Memories had a way of sneaking up on her and sliding an invisible blade between her ribs, but she struggled and eventually buried the memories deep.

"Why don't we do something fun?" Lacy suggested, kicking clumps of snow with her boots as she kept pace with Kat.

"I'm just not in the mood. Sorry." She didn't miss the wilting smile on her friend's lips. Kat would only ruin any fun Lacy would have, and a good friend wouldn't do that.

They walked through the cold stone streets in silence. Kat paused as they passed the little pub where every dream and hope she ever had about love had been born. The place where she and Tristan had first kissed. The Pickerel Inn. Now it was a reminder of what she'd loved and lost.

"We could go in." Lacy nudged her gently. "Mark's inside."

Mark, Lacy's boyfriend, was always a source of humor and good spirits, but Kat didn't want to laugh. She didn't want to feel good.

Tonight she wanted to sit in her dorm and...what? She'd done nothing but mope around the last two weeks. The logical part of her brain was shaking a finger in disgust at her own refusal to go out and have fun. However, the rest of her was in agony, so much pain that everything else was dulled to her senses.

"Kat..." Lacy wrinkled her nose and bit her lip. "You've got to shake this off. I know it's hard, but you're strong. You can survive this."

Survive without the other half of my heart? Yeah, feels pretty impossible right now.

A couple exited the pub; the woman was laughing and hugging the man's arm as they walked past Lacy and Kat.

Their happy laughter, happy intimacy, stung more than Kat could bear.

"I'm going to remember our last night at Fox Hill." Tristan's voice, so clear in her head brought a mixture of pain and joy. That was what she'd done every night since they'd parted. She'd close her eyes and focus on him, how it felt to sleep beside him, their breaths and heartbeats matched, their dreams touching deep in the night. Fingers laced together and faint butterfly kisses...

Kat glanced down at her boots and kicked some snow off their tips before she spoke.

"I need time, Lacy. You go in, and tell Mark I said hi." She didn't wait to hear if Lacy replied before starting down the snowy street. She wasn't sure how long she'd walked into the growing twilight before she had a sense she was being followed.

Stopping, she spun and saw a tall blond-haired man lounging in the doorway of a closed shop. A thick striped scarf with a school shield was draped around his neck, the ends fluttering in the light breeze. His brown eyes were assessing but not threatening. Her heart jumped.

"Carter, what are you doing here?" she whispered, relieved to see him.

"Hello, Kat." As he walked up to her, she noticed something in one of his hands. A rolled-up magazine. He held it out to her. "I think you should read this." Carter started to turn away, but she grasped his arm.

"How is he?" she asked, desperate to hear about him.

Carter raked a hand through his hair and blew out an exhausted sigh.

"Not good. I've never seen him like this." He paced away from her, like a restless beast torn with worry and anger. There was a weariness to his eyes that saddened Kat's heart. "He's cold. He's...losing himself to his grief." He spun back to face her, his eyes sweeping over her as though searching for answers. "What *happened* between you?"

"He didn't tell you?" Surprise flickered through her. Tristan and Carter shared everything. How had he not told his friend what had happened?

"Tell me what?"

"We broke up because...because of his father." She was hesitant to explain fully. If Tristan hadn't shared the details of their breakup with Carter, he must have had a reason.

"What did Pembroke do?" He crossed his arms over his chest, frowning.

"Well..." She hesitated. What could she say? Should she tell him the real reason? Would it matter?

With quick strides Carter was inches from her, hands on her shoulders as he stared down at her.

"Tell me, please, Kat. I can't help Tristan if I don't understand what we're fighting against."

What we're fighting against...His words, the sense of unity, showed just how close he and Tristan truly were. Brothers in so many ways that Tristan's father couldn't ever break them apart. Carter deserved to know the truth.

With a little nod, she sighed. "The earl used you as blackmail to keep us apart."

"Me?" Carter's eyes widened.

With a little nod, Kat explained. "His father said if we didn't end things on Christmas Day that he would fire you and your dad from the estate and make it impossible for you to be employed anywhere else. Tristan couldn't fight it. And I understood. We did what we had to in order to protect you and your father."

A tic worked in Carter's jaw as he digested this information. Then he looked at her intensely.

"So you still love him and would be with him if nothing else stood in the way?"

She nodded. "I couldn't let him hurt you or your dad. He said he'd choose me, but he shouldn't have to choose between his best friend and his girlfriend."

A slow smile curved Carter's lips. "Well, thank God for that. Why don't you go back to your dorm and read the magazine. Keep your cell phone handy. Maybe I can conjure a miracle or two before midnight." He touched her shoulder with a brotherly pat and then walked quickly away.

Kat watched him turn the corner before she headed for her dorm.

Miracles by midnight? She doubted that was possible.

With a little exhale, and a heavy heart, she returned to her room and sat on her bed. After she kicked off her boots and stripped out of her coat, she unrolled the glossy magazine Carter had handed her.

Monarch Magazine.

Her heart stuttered to a halt. Tristan was on the cover. He was seated at an antique walnut wood writing table. The photo was taken from his left and he'd put his elbows on the desk, his hands clasped together loosely as though briefly interrupted in a prayer. He faced the camera, his eyes sharp and penetrating, his full lips slightly parted, looking like he was about to say something important. The title of the article read, THE TRUTH BEHIND THE LOVE STORY SWEEPING LONDON.

Kat's heart started beating hard and fast. She wanted to stare at the photo forever. He was gloriously handsome, but there was something in his eyes that stopped her heart. An aching loneliness.

I didn't dream him. He's real. And he used to be mine.

She shut her eyes for a long moment before she found the courage to flip through the pages until she found the article. There was a huge full-page spread of the Snow White and Prince Charming kiss. She and Tristan were lip-locked and the words SOME LOVES LAST FOREVER were scrawled in an elegant font beneath their bodies. With trembling fingers she stroked the glossy page, remembering the way it had felt to come alive from a prince's kiss in a snowy glen, the sweet taste of an apple upon her lips.

She shifted her attention to the next page, where the interview began. Tristan described the way they met, how they'd kept their love a secret until his father had discovered them. Paparazzi pictures of them filled the next several pages: Tristan holding her protectively as he led her out of the registrar's office after their parents' wedding. The two of them singing at King's College, illuminated by candlelight. The two of them ice-skating.

Kat read the entire article twice before she reread the bolded quotes. There was a picture of Tristan by a window, his eyes directed out on the gardens, holding the compass she'd given him in one hand. It caught the winter sunlight and glinted sharply, like a fallen star in his palm.

She was the one thing in my life that made sense. The one thing I loved more than anything. I didn't deserve her, but somehow she loved me anyway.

Kat flipped the pages to a photo of Tristan by a fireplace, one hand on the mantel as he stared broodingly into the crackling fire's glow.

There will never be anyone else in my heart. Katherine Roberts is my only dream.

The words ripped all the wounds inside her open again, and sobs tore from her throat. She couldn't relive this pain. She couldn't.

TRISTAN RECLINED IN A CHAIR BY THE FIREPLACE IN ONE OF the drawing rooms at Pembroke. His father was waving the

Monarch Magazine around as he shouted. Tristan wasn't listening to a single word. His father looked furious enough to throw something, but he halted suddenly as the study door opened.

Carter's father, John, stood in the doorway, scowling. Usually the estate's steward was a cheery but polite and slightly reserved fellow. His blond hair was streaked with hints of silver, but his brown eyes were sharp and observant.

"What is it, John? Can't you see I'm busy?"

John walked into the room, his lean form moving with purpose. "I've come to tender my resignation. I'll be leaving within the hour and will send someone to collect my things tomorrow." His gaze stayed on the earl, but Tristan had the strangest sense that Carter's father was speaking to him. He slowly rose from the chair, his gaze darting between John and his father.

"What in the blazes do you mean, John?" Edward threw the magazine into a chair and crossed his arms, brows lowered.

Carter's father didn't back down. "It has come to my attention that you have been using me and my son to keep Tristan from dating Ms. Roberts. Well, you can trouble yourself no more. I do not hold with such low behavior. It has been an honor until today to work for such a noble family and a great house. But if you plan to run the estate through subterfuge and blackmail, then I'm done, Edward."

John turned on his heel and left the room.

Sputtering in rage and panic, Edward rushed after him. "If you think I'll let you resign, think again! I need you here, John. Come back—" The drawing room door closed, leaving Tristan alone.

Dazed, he stared at the door. Before he could process what had just happened, his cell phone rang.

"Tristan, why the bloody hell didn't you tell me!" Carter was almost shouting.

"Tell you what?" he fired back. He was unused to Carter being so...angry.

"That Edward was using me and my father as a way to keep you and Kat apart? You shouldn't have protected us, not at the cost of your own happiness. You bloody idiot. I've told Father and he's going to resign. He said he thinks your father is bluffing."

Stunned, Tristan tried to process what Carter was telling him.

"But your dad's just resigned—"

"Tristan, he won't have to, not if he can blackmail your father right back into letting you see Kat. So get in your car and drive to Cambridge. Kat needs you. Forget Edward and come back here. He can't keep you from her. There's no one stopping you anymore."

Tristan was on his feet and running for the door, pulling his keys from his pocket. He shouted for a footman to open the gates as he practically sprinted down the front steps.

The Aston Martin was still parked out front from his morning drive to the groundkeeper's lodge, which was nestled in the woods at the other end of the estate. It was dark now since twilight had faded to the onward press of night, creating a lonely, quiet atmosphere.

Just beyond the gates, a swarm of media vehicles hummed their engines to life like a hive of angry bees. Several men and women were scrambling to load cameras into cars.

He ignored them as he got into his car and gunned it toward the front gate.

"Move!" Tristan gestured through his front windshield, trying to get the cars out of his way.

"Mr. Kingsley!" one man shouted, waving his press badge, but Tristan ignored him.

Blaring his horn, he nudged his car through a narrow gap on the road between the vehicles. A few minutes later he was cruising down the road, the lights of the vehicles racing behind him on the dark road. Nothing could dull his spirits, not tonight. He used his Bluetooth to dial Kat's number. She answered on the first ring.

"Hello?" Her voice sounded stuffy, as though she had a cold.

"Darling? It's me. Are you all right?" He glanced in his rearview mirror, noticing that a black SUV had gained ground on the road behind him. He pressed his foot on the gas, easing his car up in speed.

"Tristan?" The tremor of hope in the way she breathed his name sent his heart slamming against his ribs. How he'd missed the sound of her voice.

"I'm coming to you. Carter's father attempted to resign. The old man wouldn't hear of it. There's nothing stopping us, nothing. Everything is all right. We're going to be together." And that realization filled him with joy.

A pause, and then she sniffled. "No more being apart?" Her excitement was an echo of his own.

Finally, his life was headed in a direction he wanted to go.

"No more being apart," he promised, his eyes misting, forcing Tristan to blink.

"I saw the article," Kat said, her tone soft. It was the way she'd sounded when they shared secrets in bed, opening their hearts.

"I meant every word." A silly grin curved his lips.

"How soon will you be here? Should I go out and get dinner for us?" she asked hopefully.

He glanced at the dashboard clock. "I'll be there in two hours. I'd love dinner." There was so much more he needed to say but couldn't. Not until he could do it in person.

"I'll see you soon." She laughed, the light, wonderful sound making everything right in his world again.

"I love you," he said.

"I love you, too."

Tristan pressed the disconnect button and tapped his fingers on the steering wheel, still smiling.

The SUV behind him sped up, passing him on the right. The SUV's window opened on the passenger side and a camera flashed.

Light blinded him, and he hit the brakes, trying to let the SUV past him. The paparazzi vehicle swerved closer, and he jerked the wheel to the left. The car ahead of him suddenly slammed on its brakes, and the safe distance between it and Tristan's car vanished. He clipped the bumper of the car, and the Aston Martin skidded on the ice.

His lungs seized in panic as he tried to keep the car on the road, but the ice was too slick and he slid off the pavement.

Too fast...

There was an explosion of sounds and a violent jarring just as the world turned upside down. Glass shattered and splintered, embedding in him like diamond daggers. Pain rippled through his body and he couldn't breathe. Tristan sucked at the air, helpless and hurting as numbness stole across his body. He blinked, coughed, and darkness started tunneling his vision.

Kat's face fanned out of the growing night. He was leaning over her, ready to kiss her lips. Snow fell around them, coating her lashes and cheeks. Lips petal soft beneath his...

Kat...

❧ 13 ❧

Kat checked the clock on her nightstand for the tenth time. The food she'd brought back to the dorm was cold and untouched on her desk.

Where was Tristan? He should have been here an hour ago. A creeping unease ate away at her. Why hadn't he called?

A knot formed in her stomach, and a chill stole across her skin. It was the same feeling she'd had back in London when she and Tristan had parted without a good-bye.

She dialed his cell. It rang eight times before going to voice mail. Swallowing thickly, Kat fought off the rising panic.

"Tristan, where are you? I'm worried. Please call me back when you get this." She hung up and forced herself to sit down.

Her phone rang and she jumped. "Tristan! Where are you?"

"Kat, honey, it's Dad." Her father spoke slowly, his voice strained.

"Dad, can I call you later? I'm waiting for Tristan—"

"That's why I'm calling. Honey..." An awful silence made a pit in her stomach.

"What is it, Dad?" Something bad...something *terrible* had happened, but she needed to hear him say it.

"There's been an accident."

The world shrank around her, suffocating her. *No*...

"Tristan was leaving Pembroke, and one of the paparazzi cut him off. His car rolled into a ditch. Lizzy and I are headed to the hospital. We'll call the second we know anything. I promise."

Can't breathe...Can't...She was distantly aware of someone screaming, the sound ragged and full of horrible crushing pain.

"Kat!" her father shouted, and the scream died away.

Her scream. She'd been yelling so hard her throat burned.

"Kat, breathe, honey, please. Calm down."

Her hands were shaking and she tried to focus on her father's voice and what he was saying.

"Do you know Tristan's friend Carter Martin?"

Gasping, she got out a few words. "Yes...why?"

"He's going to meet you outside your college and bring you straight to the hospital."

"Okay," she managed.

"I promise to call as soon as I know anything." Her father's voice was shaky, and that scared the hell out of her.

"Clayton, we need to leave," Lizzy said in the background.

"Coming," he said away from the cell phone, then spoke to Kat again. "I'm sure Tristan will be okay. He's a strong boy."

Yes, Tristan was strong. But a car accident...Her stomach roiled, and she clutched it.

Her dad's voice softened even more. "I've got to go, honey, but we'll call you."

"Okay." Kat barely got the one word out, then hung up.

She grabbed her coat and purse before she left her room.

The cold night air pierced her lungs as she ran down the icy sidewalk and through the front door of the college.

A black Porsche SUV was already waiting a few feet away. Celia glanced at her through the passenger window, pointing to the second row passenger side.

Kat understood and climbed in. Carter was already pulling the SUV away from the curb as she shut the door.

"We're headed to the hospital. They took him to one of the best in London." Celia turned around in her seat, a strained smile not hiding the glistening trails of tears on her cheeks.

"Is he...?" A tight lump formed in her throat.

"We don't know anything yet. He's in surgery."

Surgery. Pain lanced through Kat's entire body. *No...please no...*

"I'm sure he'll be fine." Celia's smile wilted and she turned to look at Carter. His jaw was clenched and one hand rested on the shift.

The narrow city streets became a blur as Kat tried to control her rushing thoughts. A hundred things she'd wanted to say to Tristan lingered at the edge of her mind like shadows.

Carter didn't take his eyes off the road, but he held out his left hand, palm up. Celia tucked her fingers in his. Watching them, Kat realized they loved each other, and that cut her deep all over again.

Celia and Carter didn't have any chance to be together, not like she and Tristan had. *They are more trapped than we are.*

How lucky she'd been to love Tristan for even a short while.

I want more time. I refuse to let go of him. Not till we're old and gray and lived a life together full of love. She'd never been this sure of anything in her entire life.

The two hours it took to reach the hospital were agonizing. The only moment she remembered to breathe was when Carter's phone rang.

Celia answered it and listened intently to the caller. When she hung up, she set the phone in the cup holder and sighed.

"That was Aunt Elizabeth. She said Tristan is out of surgery, and he's in a medically induced coma. There was a lot of internal bleeding, but he's stable for now. She warned us we might have trouble getting inside the hospital. Paparazzi from all over the city are waiting outside," Celia said.

"What? Why?" Kat glanced out the car windows at the London streets.

Celia's eyes widened. "You don't know? After Tristan's article in *Monarch Magazine* was published, all of London's media has been calling out Uncle Edward over the opposition to your relationship. The press are going wild with the whole love story. You two are a modern-day Romeo and Juliet. Everyone is rooting for you to get back together. Tristan is a hero and you the luckiest girl in England, at least that's what the *Daily Mail* said." Celia checked her phone again for the tenth time since they'd left Cambridge.

Romeo and Juliet? We are just as star-crossed, Kat thought. She'd noticed the building press in Cambridge but hadn't thought it had anything to do with her and Tristan until Carter had shown her the article in *Monarch*.

"Are you sure we'll be able to get into the hospital?" Kat asked.

Carter growled softly. "We'll find a way in."

Yes, we will, Kat vowed. No one would stop her.

When they reached the hospital, they saw hundreds of people lining the sidewalks. Everyone in the crowd held little candles. The night fell around the streets, but the hundreds of candles danced like fireflies on a summer's night. If her heart hadn't been breaking, Kat would have been mesmerized by the sight.

"Celia, take Kat inside, I'll see to the car and join you in a few minutes."

Celia leaned over in the seat, her lashes lowering as she brushed a kiss to his cheek, and then she got out of the car. Kat followed her. Celia slipped one arm through hers, as though needing the strength.

We'll lean on each other.

"It's her!" someone called from in the crowd. Dozens of faces close to Kat turned her way. Cameras started appearing and bodies started to pack between her and the door. But she wasn't going to let them stop her. She had to find Tristan.

"Please!" she shouted. "Let me through!" For a long moment nothing happened, and she feared she'd have to start shoving people away.

Finally, after an agonizing pause, cameras slowly lowered and the reporters backed away, forming a clear path to the hospital door.

She and Celia hurried past the watchful crowd, the candlelight casting shadows against their faces and the hospital exterior.

"This way." Celia guided Kat to a bay of elevators.

As they rode up the few floors to the ICU, Kat could barely think beyond that she was helpless to do anything for Tristan.

At the end of a long white-walled hall, she spotted her father and Lizzy huddled by an open doorway. A few feet apart from them stood Edward Kingsley.

"Dad!" Kat tore free of Celia's gentle hold and ran to her father.

He held one arm out, catching her as she threw herself at him.

Every pain fracturing inside her chest seemed to intensify.

"Shh...It's okay, honey. Everything will be okay."

Kat almost believed him, but when she rubbed the tears

from her eyes and turned to look through the open door, everything inside her stilled.

Tristan lay in the hospital bed, one leg in a cast. His face was a little bruised, with a few cuts on his cheekbones and chin. His head was fine except for a patch of white bandage by his right ear.

"They were able to reduce the swelling, and the internal bleeding has stopped. He's still in a medically induced coma, but they're hoping he'll wake soon." Her father's voice seemed so distant, as though he spoke to her from another world just out of reach.

She took a step toward Tristan, but a hand jerked her to a halt. It was Edward Kingsley.

❧ 14 ❧

"He's lying there because of you. Haven't you done enough?" Edward's eyes were wide, wild, and a range of emotions, from anger to pain, all sparked and churned as he stared at Kat. She dropped her gaze to where his hand was curled around her arm in a viselike grip. He released her with a soft growl. His face was etched with lines of pain, and his eyes were too bright, as though he was fighting off tears. This wasn't the monster she'd wanted to believe he was. This was a man hurting for his child. It didn't erase his mean-spirited treatment, but it made him human.

Her heart, beating, aching, opened wide inside her, and she reacted without thinking. She hugged Tristan's father.

He muttered something but didn't push her away. When she stepped back, he swallowed thickly and met her gaze.

"I love him. I'm not leaving. I don't know what I can do, but..." Her voice faltered, and more tears pooled in her eyes. What else could she say?

She went into Tristan's room and pulled up a chair by his bed. His right hand lay close to her, and she curled her fingers around his, squeezing. She wasn't sure how long she sat there, monitors beeping softly in the background, memorizing Tristan's features, the way his dark hair fell into his closed eyes.

Kat was flooded with too many emotions and a thousand thoughts that moved through her with tidal force, pulling her along to one steady burning realization. She couldn't live without him, and she would do everything in her power to help him survive this.

Come back to me. Find your way home.

She parted her dry lips and spoke, hoping her words would reach Tristan in whatever twilight world he was trapped in. "From the moment I met you, I loved you." She smiled through her tears. "Even then I recognized you as my other half. I never thought soul mates existed, but when we kissed...It was like something inside of me unlocked a secret place in my heart just for you. Do you hear me, Tristan? That's only for you. No one else." She stroked her thumb on the side of his palm as she talked on.

I would do anything for you. You woke me up from a dream and taught me to live...to love.

"Please, Tristan. Find your way home to me."

Hours passed, but Kat was aware only of Tristan and the monitors that showed no changes in his vital signs besides an indication he was still asleep. She continued to talk until her voice grew hoarse.

"Here." A gruff voice interrupted her exhausted thoughts. Edward was standing beside her, a plastic cup in his hand.

She glanced up in surprise.

"You'll get hoarse if you keep on and don't have some water." He pressed the cup into her free hand.

Kat drank it, the cool water a balm to her raw throat. She set it on the little table and glanced at the doorway.

"Where's—"

"Your father took Elizabeth to the empty room next door to rest. She's exhausted. I promised I would stay with Tristan and if he started to wake, I'd get them." Edward walked around to the opposite side of the bed and seated himself in the other chair, then with a little exhale, reached out and touched Tristan's other hand.

Edward didn't speak for a long while. He sat in stony silence, his mouth forming a hard, angry line.

"Talk to him. It will help him to hear your voice. Please," she begged softly. "We both love him."

When Edward finally tore his gaze from Tristan to stare at her, there was less anger and more sadness in his eyes.

"It's not that I don't like you. I just believe my son should be marrying someone who..." He paused, and Kat finished his sentence.

"Someone you approve of? Or someone you can use for a political advantage? Oh, I understand, Mr. Kingsley."

He laughed bitterly. "That is just it. You don't even know to call me Lord Pembroke."

She fought off the need to bristle at his exasperated sigh. "I can learn to be what Tristan needs me to be. I'm not afraid, *Lord* Pembroke. Is that your only objection to me? That I'm not a British aristocrat?"

Tristan's father was studying her intently now, and she sat very still beneath his intense scrutiny.

"I have plenty of objections, but I have a feeling you'll argue against all of them. Typical American behavior." He stayed silent for another minute and then shook his head. "At least the media likes you. I saw the article, of course. The two of you ice-skating, singing at church. I don't think Tristan's been inside a church in years..." As Edward opened up about Tristan, the anger in him seemed to be slightly diffused. "I had no idea he could skate. I don't know when he learned to do that. We never took him skating as a boy. He doesn't do things like that with other women, just you." He was still staring at her.

Kat swallowed, unsure what to say to that. "Would you tell me about when you used to take him to the Kensington Gardens? He told me it was one of his happiest memories."

"He said that?" Edward's brows raised.

She nodded.

A hint of a smile curved Edward's lips. "The boy always had so much energy. Best to get him up and running about." He chuckled. "He was quite a scamp."

Kat kissed Tristan's hand as she listened to his father talk.

"Did you know he had a wild imagination as a boy? Always playacting with Carter. The two of them never stayed out of trouble for long." Edward shook his head, still smiling.

"Carter is like a brother to him," Kat said. "I think, one day, they'll make Pembroke a wonderful place. He has so many ideas—" She halted, not wanting to anger Edward or get Tristan in more trouble with his father.

Edward stared at his son, but when he spoke the words were for her.

"Ideas? What sort of ideas?" Rather than sound upset, his tone was gentle, almost curious.

"He wants to make Pembroke a place where people will come from all over the world to visit. He thinks if you allow some film crews on the grounds to use it for period dramas, it'll make the estate famous," Kat explained. She detailed Tristan's plans and watched Edward, expecting the building storm again, but it didn't come.

"Tristan told you his plans? I admit when he first told me I wasn't thrilled with the idea but it has grown on me these last few weeks." Surprise colored the earl's voice.

"Yes. He was so excited about it. He and Carter have it all mapped out..." She paused. "Did you fire Carter and his father?"

Edward finally looked at her. "No. I would never sack them, no matter what I said. John tried to resign, but he reminded me, well...that we were more than a team. Long ago, we were friends. I'd forgotten that somehow, in the last thirty years." Lines of worry carved into his face and he scrubbed his jaw. "So...you love my son." He seemed to be speaking more to himself than to her, but she replied anyway.

"Yes. I tried so many times not to love him. I promised to stay away from him, but it's like..."

"Like you're the sea and he's the shore? You always come crashing back to each other by forces greater than you can understand." Edward glanced at Tristan. His lips quivered and a tear rolled down his cheek.

With a muttered apology, the man wiped away the evidence of his emotions.

"Who was it...?" Kat could barely get the words out. "Who did you love so completely like that?" She knew deep in her soul that this man understood them more than she'd ever imagined someone could.

Edward closed his eyes, exhaled, and then looked out the window at the dark, sleeping city. Their reflections on the glass from the hall lights made them appear to be frozen phantoms.

"Her name was Lydia. Her family lived on the estate and worked as part of the household staff. My father never knew she and I...how we felt about each other. I knew if he discovered us, he'd send her family away."

Kat covered Tristan's hand with both of hers, holding on to him as she listened to his father open his heart and expose his painful past.

"What happened to Lydia?"

Edward's head lowered a few inches. "John Martin came to work for my father. He was my age. Twenty-four. He took over as steward and met Lydia. There was nothing standing between them. No grand house, no titles, no traditions. I stood next to John in the church the day of their wedding. A man's heart can break and not kill him, I found out as I watched them get married." Edward didn't wipe the second tear away as it coursed down his cheek.

"What about Tristan's mother?" Kat asked, almost afraid of the pain the question might cause, but needing to know.

"She came into my life a few weeks after the wedding. She was like Lydia in so many ways, but she was never mine, not like Lydia had been. Every hurt I've suffered since I lost Lydia, I took out on Elizabeth…" He didn't finish, but it wasn't necessary.

"The world is different now," Kat whispered. "Tristan and I can be together." She held her breath, waiting to see what Edward would say.

"Much has changed in thirty years," he agreed.

Several long moments passed while Kat and Edward kept a vigilant watch on Tristan's condition.

Then at last Edward spoke.

"Why don't you try to rest? I shall stay with him for a few hours." Edward shifted in his chair as though settling in for a long watch.

"No," Kat whispered. "I won't leave. I made a promise, one I've broken too many times. I was *always* the one who gave up on us because I was too afraid of what I felt for him. I'm never going to hurt him again." Thick tears blurred her eyes enough that she had trouble seeing. She blinked rapidly, sending the tears trickling down her cheeks.

The hospital monitors beeped away, steady and unchanging, measuring the silence in the room by the slow beat of Tristan's heart.

"Then sleep here. I'll watch him if he wakes." Edward's suggestion was the only option she could accept.

Every muscle in her body ached. Worry and fear had drained her to the point where she couldn't fight sleep. Scooting her chair closer, Kat rested her elbows on Tristan's bed and folded her arms so she could lay her head on them. She kept hold of his hand, unwilling to lose that connection to him.

She slipped into that twilight place between wakefulness and sleep. Dreams of him came to her, one at a time in shimmering incandescent waves that blinded her with their brilliance. His arms about her, his lips feathering over hers, the way his eyes sparkled as he laughed. She loved how he talked of his dreams for the future with such hope. The way he spoke of Celia and Carter with such affection. Tristan was so much more than the charming womanizer the press painted him as. He was a loyal friend, irresistible lover, a man with dreams to build a greater life for those in his world.

Lost in her own dreams, Kat didn't immediately feel the gentle pressure on her hand. She came awake slowly, convinced she'd imagined it. Bleary-eyed, she glanced at the clock above the bed. Two hours had passed. She peeked at Edward, who was still watching Tristan, weary but awake.

There it was again, that hint of pressure.

Kat squeezed back, staring hard at Tristan's face for any sign of him coming around.

A flicker of his lids, a tensing of his jaw. Surely I can't be imagining this.

His fingers tightened around hers, the sensation clearly recognizable now. Her heart leaped into her throat and she gasped breathlessly.

"Take his other hand. He's waking up. I have to get Lizzy and Dad!" She jumped up, waited impatiently for Edward to do as she ordered, and then she rushed out of the room to get Lizzy.

Tristan was waking up at last.

133

THEY SAY LIFE FLASHES THROUGH A PERSON'S EYES WHEN they're about to die. But no one says anything about the moments before you come back to life. This was the hazy thought that lay at the back of Tristan's mind as he watched the play of images and sensations roll through his mind.

The light glinting off the top of Peter Pan's flute in a garden, the feel of his father's arms catching him, both of them laughing. The bright colors from a stained-glass window of a knight and his lady. Chasing Carter through the woods, laughing as they followed the groundskeeper to collect grouse eggs. The bite of a winter's night and the hot kiss of a girl with silver eyes. The flutter of a butterfly against his cheek as he leaned in for one more kiss, one last taste. The glow of winter sunlight on an antique compass in his hand, the arrow pointing him toward his future...toward her.

"Kat." The name came out a rough, raspy whisper that scraped his ears.

"I'm here." Her voice was so clear, so real. Was he still dreaming?

"Kat?" Tristan coughed, and suddenly pain flared inside every cell of his body. His eyelids scratched against his eyes like sandpaper as he forced them open. Everything was blurry, and he had to blink a few times.

A group of people were huddled around him. His father, his mother, Clayton, Celia, Carter...and Kat. *His Kat.*

"You're here," he whispered. The other people in the room vanished, and he saw only her. A hundred emotions smashed into him and tears burned his eyes because he was too bloody weak to get up and take the woman he loved into his arms.

Kat bit her lip and nodded, tears streaming down her face. Her dark hair fell about her face in wild waves, as though she'd been running her hands through it in worried distraction.

She was still beautiful.

"Yes, I'm here, and I'm not going anywhere," she promised.

Hearing that made his entire body relax, and yet he still needed to hold her.

He struggled to sit up, but his father touched his shoulder gently. "Easy, boy. Plenty of time for that later."

Tristan glanced at Edward, blinking slowly. His father's eyes were red-rimmed. *Why?*

"Father, what—"

"Shhh..." His mother hushed him. "Don't speak. Just rest. We're all here and so glad you're all right."

The heavy weight of his head was too much to hold up. He let it drop back onto his pillow, his eyes falling closed again, but he was afraid Kat would leave once he was lost to sleep again.

"Kat, don't go." Tristan squeezed her hand, and sighed in relief when she squeezed back.

"I'm right here. Not going to anywhere." The faint press of her lips on his forehead filled him with an intense, overwhelming joy. He exhaled a happy, exhausted breath.

"We...belong together." He kept a hold on her hand.

"Yes, we do. Sleep now, my prince." Her soft laugh was in his ears. "I'll wake you with a kiss."

He smiled as he drifted off. The message from the stained glass at Fox Hill came back to him.

Love conquers all.

❧ 15 ❧

Five *months later at the Pembroke estate...*

"I can't concentrate when you do that thing," Kat murmured as electric tingles shot down her spine.

"What thing?" Tristan's voice rumbled against her ear as he folded her into his embrace from behind.

"That thing...with your tongue." She rolled up on her tiptoes, breathless and flushing with heat as he licked the shell of her ear before he nibbled on the sensitive spot behind it.

"Classes are over, darling. It's summer. Come and play with me," Tristan suggested, his hands sliding down her hips and playing with the skirt of the sky-blue sundress she wore.

Kat closed her eyes, leaning back against him. She never had the power to resist Tristan once he touched her. Spark meet tinder. She laughed softly. There would always be an unquenchable fire between them.

"The party starts in an hour," she said. "I need to memorize the forms of address for the peers attending today, or I'll embarrass you and upset your dad."

He exhaled softly against her neck, then spun her around to face him.

"All you have to do is follow my lead. As for my father... well..." Tristan's lips twisted into a wry smile. "I think you've done the impossible and won the old bastard over. I don't know how, but I believe he's starting to like you." The bemused and puzzled look on Tristan's face made Kat smile.

She reached up to trace his lips with her fingertips. He kissed the pads of her fingers, his blue-green eyes bright and glowing.

It never ceased to amaze Kat how fortunate she was. She'd come so close to losing him in January. Seeing him broken and bruised in that hospital had almost destroyed her, but he'd pulled through. If not for the small scar behind one ear, no one would guess he'd survived a near-fatal car wreck.

"What are you thinking about?" Tristan asked, tilting her chin up so he could better see her face.

She grasped his wrist, squeezing lightly as she smiled. "I was just thinking how lucky I am that you're okay, after the wreck."

Shadows flitted across his beautiful eyes. "I'm here, and I'm fine." It was a promise he'd made so many times in the months that followed the accident, but she never got tired of hearing it.

"I know." Kat walked into his arms. She could feel his heat through the three-piece navy blue suit he wore. When she pressed her cheek against his chest, the steady *thump-thump* of his heart was a comforting sound. His woodsy, clean male scent, with a hint of pine, filled her nose, and she rubbed her face against him.

"Ahem." A cool voice cut through the quiet, perfect moment. Tristan's father stood, rigid as always, in the doorway to Tristan's bedroom.

"Yes?" Tristan's tone was just as cool, but lacking the edge it used to have.

Since the accident things had changed.

"When you and Katherine are done canoodling like a pair of doves, Carter and Celia need help setting place cards on the tables outside. Elizabeth and Clayton are outside, as well, as you both should be." He raised one brow in challenge at Tristan, then turned to Kat. "See that he wears his coat, Katherine. I expect you to make him look presentable."

"Of course, my lord," Kat said, heat suffusing her cheeks. Whenever Tristan's father spoke to her now, she always expected him to be cruel, and was continually surprised he was doing just what Tristan said.

He's really warming up to me.

"Very good." Edward nodded once and left them alone.

Tristan growled, but there was no bite to the sound. "One of these days I'm going to put a collar with a bell on him so he can't keep sneaking up on us like that."

Kat giggled and leaned up to kiss Tristan. "He's rather like an old English ninja, isn't he?"

"Bloody nuisance, more like." Tristan walked over to the bedroom door and closed it, sliding the lock firmly into place. He rolled the cuff back on his left wrist to examine his watch, then raised his gaze to hers, mischief glinting in his eyes.

"I think I can get inside you and make you come in less than five minutes. Time enough before the old man expects us to be downstairs greeting guests. What say you to that, little stepsister?" He winked devilishly.

"Oh, no!" Kat raised her hands up to keep him away, but her body was already humming with desire. Being with Tristan was like being near an ever-burning flame. Her body's hunger for him was only temporarily sated but never extinguished.

"Oh, yes!" He stalked toward her, cutting a fine figure in

his suit. Tall, lean, too sexy for his own good, his dark hair tousled from his hands running through it.

"We can't. You'll mess up my dress." Kat's excuse was only halfhearted, as she tried to skirt around the bed.

"Perhaps a bit, but you won't mind, not after I'm done fucking you, sweet Kat." He uttered the words low and deliciously smooth, in that tone that always made her knees buckle.

When he caught up with her on the other side of the bed, Tristan pinned her wrists against the wall above her head with one hand and kissed her ruthlessly. Then he dropped his other hand to tease the hem of her skirt, stroking her outer thigh.

"We have all the time in the world," he whispered against her lips, and little shivers shot through her.

With a brazen little chuckle, she replied, "But I don't want to waste it talking."

The rich heat in his gaze and the fire of their lips coming together scorched her clear through.

Drawn together by invisible forces, they would never be apart. They wanted to face their destiny together, whatever it might be.

"I love you," he whispered between slow, deep, drugging kisses. He pressed his forehead against hers.

"I love you, too." They were no longer words that tore at Kat's heart; rather, they gave her the strength to fly.

Behind Tristan on the opposite wall hung the poster of their kiss at the Harrods department store photo shoot. It felt like only yesterday when he'd woken her with a kiss, and their lives would never be the same.

Once upon a time...I fell in love with Tristan Kingsley, a future earl, my stepbrother, the man who believed our love would conquer all...and he was right.

EPILOGUE

Carter Martin lingered at the edge of the gardens, watching the crowds flutter about the tables. Champagne glasses were never left empty, and the gossip mills were churning. But the topics were lighter this time than they had been in the past. Things had changed since London had embraced Tristan and Kat as their darling couple. A love that would last, a fairy tale.

Stifling a chuckle, he smoothed his gray suit vest and checked his cuffs before he stepped out into the sunlight, escaping the shadows of the grand country house. He caught sight of Tristan and Kat as they strolled arm in arm toward Clayton and Elizabeth.

Everything was right in their world now, all smiles and sunshine. An all-too-familiar pang of envy stung him, filtering his world in shades of green. He would never know such peace or joy. Not when the one thing in the world he craved beyond all else was far out of his reach.

He ran his hands through his hair, tugging hard at the strands until the pain brought him back down to the ground.

"Carter?" A feminine voice dragged up from the depths of

his buried desire stole his breath. He spun around to face the doorway to the servants' quarters he'd slipped out of only a few minutes before.

Celia Lynton stood there in a beautiful red gown with a deep V-neck that showed off her collarbone.

Lord, he'd imagined kissing that place a thousand times, desperate to know if it was sensitive.

When his gaze lifted to her face, he nearly stumbled back. Her eyes were red-rimmed and her lips were trembling.

"Celia?" He uttered her name hoarsely. "What's the matter?"

Rather than answer him, she reached out, grabbed his tie, and dragged him into the house, slamming the door shut behind them. The sounds of the party were muted, and the servants' quarters were dim except for a distant light from the other end of the hall. Carter grabbed her shoulders, feeling her soft bare skin beneath his palms. It took everything in him not to lose control.

"I've been seeing Lord Cavanaugh's son on and off for the last couple of months. It wasn't serious, not to me." Her hesitation struck him deep.

"Celia, what is it? Talk to me," he urged gently even though his entire body was coiled tight as a metal spring ready to snap.

"He proposed today. My parents overhead. They're already talking about announcing the engagement in a few weeks." Shadows darkened beneath her eyes as she glanced down at her feet.

Carter swallowed thickly. He and Tristan had been friends with the Duke of Cavanagh's son, Callum Radcliffe, at Eton, but Callum had chosen Oxford over Cambridge, and they hadn't seen much of one another since then. Mostly because Carter didn't attend the social functions a duke's son would.

The party being held at Pembroke was, of course, an exception.

"Did you...say yes?" He asked the question even though the answer terrified him.

Celia stared deep into his eyes, then slowly shook her head. "I didn't. It all happened so fast. Mum and Dad were there, talking over me. I never actually agreed, but it's too late. They're setting everything in motion, and it's impossible to get out of it. Poor Callum," she whispered. A stray tear trickled down her cheek.

"Poor Callum?" Carter growled, and her eyes widened as she gazed up at him. "What about you? You're not doing this, Celia. Tell me you'll stop it. He's a nice bloke, but you can't marry him. You don't love him."

Her laugh was hollow. "Since when has love ever been much of a choice?"

Throwing a glance out through the windows by the servants' door, he nodded at the party. Kat and Tristan were dancing together, laughing.

"If they can...we can."

Tears frosted her brown lashes like diamond dust, and it punched him in the gut.

"I can't do that, Carter. I'm not..." She sucked in a little sob. "Uncle Edward supports Tristan's choice now, but neither of my parents will come around, not now that Callum's proposed. He's going to be a duke! My father's always wanted me to marry up. I can't get out of this. I just want—" She wiped at her eyes. "I want to be with you, just for a little while before it ends."

She didn't have to say what *it* was. She meant her happiness.

"Tell me what I can do to help," he whispered as she sidled a step closer. Her natural essence enveloped him, drugging him with its feminine aroma. There was a hint of something sweet, like wild orchids, too, a delicate perfume she used on rare occasions. The scent always imprinted upon him when she was near.

She swallowed thickly, tilted her chin up, and stared at him, eyes bright with a flash of panic.

"I asked my father if I could visit my aunt Holly for a month. She lives in Tuscany during the summer. I thought...Well, would you come with me?" Celia reached for his hands and clasped them in her own. The intimate touch was so unexpected but so welcome. The first time had been when...*we were twelve and we'd hidden in a tree house the groundskeeper built for Tristan.* The last time had been when they were racing to the hospital, praying Tristan would survive his injuries from the car wreck.

"Celia." He exhaled slowly, every muscle inside him coiled tight with a need to drag her into his arms. "Your father would never—"

She pressed a fingertip to his lips, silencing him. "He won't know. Please, Carter."

It would be their last chance. Their *only* chance. The words hung unspoken between them.

To be with Celia. It was his dream, ever since he'd been a boy. Every thought, every action, they were all for her. How could he deny her anything she wished? How could he deny his own heart?

He lowered his head and pressed his lips to hers. The time for waiting was over. If his life were a fairy tale like Tristan's, his would be *Cinderella*, the clock ticking faster and faster until the magic vanished at the stroke of midnight and he'd be left alone in a kitchen of cinders, a prince no more.

Her lips were soft and her face wet with her tears. He'd never kissed a woman who'd just been crying moments before.

"Everything is going to be all right. I promise," he

murmured against her lips. It was the first kiss in a long time that made his head a little fuzzy and a cottony warmth spread from his heart outward. She shivered in his arms, as though nervous and a little frightened, but her lips were smiling against his. They hadn't kissed since they were fourteen. So much had changed, and it was as though he was learning about her lips all over again.

When they broke apart, he stroked her cheeks with the pads of his thumbs and she clasped his wrists with her hands, clinging to him.

"What time do we leave?" he asked.

Celia bit her bottom lip, then replied. "As soon as the party is over."

A month...Well, classes were over, but could he leave his father alone to tend to the estate?

"What's the matter?" Celia whispered.

"It's my father. He has so much to take care of. If I leave him for that long..." He closed his eyes for a brief instant before opening them again.

"Tell Tristan, no one else. He can help us. I *know* he'll help us." She cupped his face and stood up on her tiptoes to feather her lips over his again.

The kiss, although light, sent bolts of violent hunger shooting through his body. His hands grasped her waist, dragging her to him as he deepened the kiss. Carter knew in that moment he could never get enough of her.

"You're right. He will help us." Tristan was his best friend and knew more than anyone else what it was like to love someone forbidden.

"I have to go." Celia's gaze darted around. "I'll meet you at the airport tomorrow morning. I'll text you the gate. My father is letting me take the private jet." She squeezed his hand one more time, but he ached for her to kiss him. Her sad little smile told him what he already knew. If they kissed again, they might not be able to stop.

"See you soon." He watched her vanish out of the servants' entrance, back into the party. He collapsed against the wall. Dropping his head back, Carter focused on breathing and calming down. Tomorrow he was going to Italy with Celia. For an entire month, just the two of them.

Tick-tock, tick-tock.

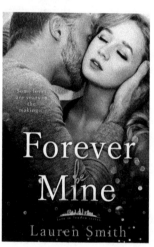

Stay tuned for Carter and Celia's Story, *Forever Be Mine*! Coming soon! To find out when it releases follow me on at least one of these places below!

**Join my Newsletter:
http://laurensmithbooks.com/free-books-and-newsletter/**

Follow Me on BookBub:
https://www.bookbub.com/authors/lauren-smith

Join my Facebook VIP Reader Group called Lauren Smith's League:
https://www.facebook.com/groups/400377546765661/

ABOUT THE AUTHOR

USA TODAY Bestselling Author Lauren Smith is an Oklahoma attorney by day, who pens adventurous and edgy romance stories by the light of her smart phone flashlight app. She knew she was destined to be a romance writer when she attempted to re-write the entire *Titanic* movie just to save Jack from drowning. Connecting with readers by writing emotionally moving, realistic and sexy romances no matter what time period is her passion. She's won multiple awards in several romance subgenres including: New England Reader's Choice Awards, Greater Detroit Book-Seller's Best Awards, and a Semi-Finalist award for the Mary Wollstonecraft Shelley Award.

To connect with Lauren, visit her at:
www.laurensmithbooks.com
lauren@Laurensmithbooks.com

facebook.com/LaurenDianaSmith

twitter.com/LSmithAuthor

instagram.com/LaurenSmithbooks

bookbub.com/authors/lauren-smith

CPSIA information can be obtained
at www.ICGtesting.com
Printed in the USA
FSHW010820280519
58491FS